# Across the Creek

## Takeaways

# Across the Creek

## Rosanne Hawke

Lothian
BOOKS

*For James Trevilyan*

### Acknowledgements
Thank you to the following for their helpful ideas: the students of Bute and Wallaroo Primary Schools, especially Brendan Bettess and Stephanie Noble; Tom Shapcott, Leanne Gates, Janeen Brian; to Jenice Loechel for the use of her name, and to my editor Gwenda.

Thomas C. Lothian Pty Ltd
132 Albert Road, South Melbourne, Victoria 3205
www.lothian.com.au

Copyright © Rosanne Hawke 2004
First published 2004

National Library of Australia
Cataloguing-in-publication data:

Hawke, Rosanne.
Across the creek.

For children aged 8–10 years.

ISBN 0 7344 0625 8 (pbk.)

1. Missing children – Juvenile fiction.
1. Title. (Series : Takeaways).

A823.3

Cover and text illustrations by Marc McBride
Cover design by Michelle Mackintosh
Book design by Paulene Meyer
Printed in Australia by Griffin Press

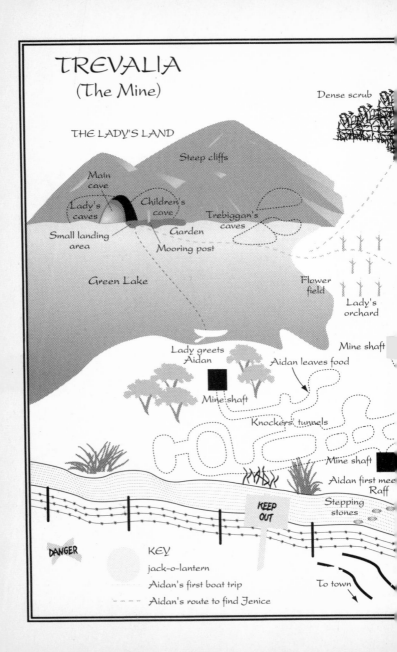

Dry plain
(Epa-tura haze)

Low scrub

Mine chimney

Rocks

Hedley sees jack-o'-lanterns

N

W                    E

S

DARK BUSH

Spriggans'
orchard

Mine/shaft

Aidan sees
jack-o'-lanterns

DANGER

Spriggans'
underground
caves

Spriggans'
cave

Children's
cave

DANGER

Scrub

Creek

Dragaroo's cave

Barbed-wire fence

# One

Aidan knew he shouldn't wander alone near the abandoned mine, especially not to the creek where Jenice Trengove disappeared last year. It was as if the water was calling him, 'Ai-dan. Ai-dan'. It sounded like hundreds of tiny voices singing without words, slow as in a dream. And just as in a dream (though Aidan was sure it wasn't) he climbed down the bank, past the 'Keep Out' sign and through the barbed wire to the water. That was where he hesitated — his moment of 'should I or shouldn't I?' He felt a quiver in his belly as if something with lots of legs was uncurling in there. Did Jenice do this last year? Ever since she disappeared, the mine and the creek had been fenced off. There were danger signs on the other side. He twisted to glance behind him but the voices called louder, like a musical waterfall. 'Ai-dan.' It sounded as though it came from the mine.

Aidan hopped from stone to stone across the sunken creek to the low scrub on the other side. Just as his foot touched dry grass, he felt a scratch on his ankle. Something was there, clinging onto his sneaker. 'Get away!' Aidan tried to shake it off. What was it anyway? It had round eyes, a wide grinning mouth and pointed ears too big for its head; weird green clothes and a little green cap like a beanie. It couldn't be human, it was far too small.

'Gotcha now, boy.' The thing wrapped its skinny arms around Aidan's leg all the tighter and laughed. 'We've been waiting for you.' Aidan was so shocked to hear it talk that he started to stutter. He hadn't done that for years.

'W-what are you?'

''Tis a piskey I am, you ignorant boy. Raff be my name. We be living here in the mine, across the water.'

'Piss-key? What a weird name.' Aidan was still trying to shift the thing off his leg. He was surprised the little thing didn't answer. It suddenly let go and stood tall, as high as Aidan's shin, and listened, one little hand cupped behind its pointed ear.

'Quickly! Something be coming. 'Tis not a safe place to be.' And with that the piskey pulled one of Aidan's shoelaces undone and dragged him further into the scrub, past rusted danger signs and into deeper grass. The piskey was still laughing but the sound had a sharp edge to it.

'Come on. Faster, boy, faster! Don't run like a crab.' Aidan tried to do what he was told, but it was difficult running with a weird little thing flying just above the ground, pulling you by the shoelace. It was worse than three-legged races at school.

'Were you always here? Across the creek?' Aidan puffed, thinking of Jenice Trengove.

'From Cornwall we came. On a ship long ago.'

Aidan didn't think he'd ever get used to the singsong way Raff spoke, and the laughing. It made him think of water falling over rocks on a sweltering day.

'Dug up, this land were, and its first dwellers gone.'

'Who —?'

'Shhh! Spriggan spit!' All of a sudden the piskey stopped flying and hovered near the ground like a huge green bee; Aidan almost stepped on top of him.

'What's wrong?' Then Aidan felt a tremor beneath his feet. Either it was an earthquake, or something gigantic was slowly thumping towards them.

'Too late. Too late! The danger is upon us.' And Raff flew up to Aidan's shoulder. Aidan could feel him fluttering. His wings were tickling his ear.

'What danger?' Aidan peered between the stringy mulga bushes, and suddenly he was as still as a rock. 'W–what's *that*?' He stared at the creature advancing on them; it had a red body with huge red and white flapping wings, a tail longer than a crocodile's. In front was a baby one almost as big as Aidan, hanging out of a pouch. The mother swayed from side to side as though it was just learning to walk. Then suddenly it paused, reared back its head and shot a tongue of flames at Aidan's feet. He leapt aside just in time.

'A dragaroo, 'tis.' The piskey was shaking so much his beanie was slipping off.

'Well, do something,' Aidan shouted. 'Don't just flap and flutter.'

'I can't,' Raff wailed. 'Once I've been seen when I didn't want to be, I have no magic powers.' He wasn't laughing now.

'I don't care about magic.' Aidan picked up a stick. 'We're having a barbecue tonight and I want to be back for it.'

Raff started to moan and flap all the more as the dragaroo waddled closer, almost tripping over its tail which coiled in front. It reminded Aidan of a huge digging machine he saw at a building site once.

'Be you blind as a bat, boy? We'll be the barbecue.' Raff hovered uncertainly in the air above Aidan.

'No, we won't.' Aidan lunged forward with

his stick like Zorro in the movie. It didn't work. The dragaroo was closer now — it grabbed the stick end in its claws and Aidan felt himself slithering towards the open jaws of the baby dragaroo.

'Oh boy, you be finished. So soon. So soon! And the job not done.'

Aidan let go just in time but he was too close. The mother could pick him up any time now. Its head slowly loomed down. Its nostrils snorted red goo, its eyes were huge and unblinking.

'Run, boy!'

But Aidan couldn't run — the dragaroo was right there. He could feel the heat coming from its mouth. Surely it could stretch out one claw and pin him to the ground? In desperation, he squeezed his eyes shut and grabbed two handfuls of dust and threw them up at those glaring eyes as high and as hard as he could. Bingo! The dragaroo reared up, staggered and screeched, its claws scraped at its face.

'Good shot, boy,' Raff shouted. 'Now, run!'

This time the piskey flew onto Aidan's shoulder as the boy crashed back through the scrub to the creek.

'You will come again?' Raff rose into the air and hung there like a tiny helicopter stalling. His mouth turned down as Aidan stepped out onto the first stone. 'We need you. You must be coming back. Besides, you haven't seen everything yet — not even the green lake. Nor have you tasted magic food.'

Aidan shook his head. 'No thanks,' and he darted off across the creek without looking behind him. At least he knew now what happened to Jenice Trengove, though he doubted anyone would believe him.

# Two

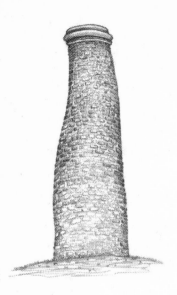

As the days passed Aidan couldn't shift Raff out of his head. It was as if the piskey was in there talking: 'Come back. We need you.' What could Aidan do? It was like a strange new country across the creek. He was sure no one knew about it.

'Aren't you coming to the oval for a kick?'

Aidan looked up to see Josh. He shook his head.

'You crook or something?' Josh crouched beside him. 'You never miss a game.'

'Just thinking.'

'What about?'

Aidan sighed. 'What do you think really happened to Jenice?'

They both stared at the fountain in the middle of the yard — the one the school council put there last year when Jenice wasn't found. *In memory of Jenice Trengove, who was lost in the bush but never lost to us.* Aidan knew it by heart.

'All those search parties — on the news, everything — and they never found a thing.'

'Yeah,' Josh said, 'even my uncle didn't find anything and he can track an ant on cement.'

'So what did he say about it?'

'She fell in the creek.'

'There was no body.'

'I know. My uncle said it was weird …'

'What happened? He thinks someone took her?'

'Nah — he wouldn't say. She wasn't the only one, you know. Chris Jones's grandpa reckons his uncle William disappeared the same way — when the uncle was a kid. Long time ago, more than a hundred years.'

Aidan glanced at Josh before he said the next bit. 'You ever heard of piskeys? They're playful, like jokes?' He said it carelessly as if he didn't care about it.

'*Piss*-keys? You kidding?' Josh laughed. 'If Miss Lawless hears you saying rude words, Aidan, you'll get detention.'

Aidan didn't smile. 'Mum's always going on about telling her where I'll be and staying put if I get bushed. Maybe Jenice did just get lost in the scrub.'

Aidan didn't tell Josh he missed Jenice. She used to come to his cubby when Mrs Trengove was having coffee with his mum. He and Jenice wrote secret messages and buried them — set up treasure hunts too. She didn't like footy but she was still fun, swinging her pigtails and laughing, like that time she climbed up onto the roof of his cubby and helped pull him up too. 'C'mon, don't be a scaredy cat,' she had shouted. She was older than him by half a year and bigger. 'We're the kings of the world up here.' Aidan had never thought to climb on top of his cubby before. It was fun; Jenice was always fun. And she helped drag him home that day he fell off the Ross Creek bridge. She may have saved his life. There was no way he could imagine Jenice at the bottom of the creek.

# Three

That day after school Aidan saw Mrs Trengove with a basket doing her shopping in the local supermarket. She didn't do it like Aidan's mum, bouncy, smiling at the girl behind the checkout. No, Mrs Trengove dragged herself around the store, picking up a pear, putting it back down, and she didn't even look at the toys or school snacks. Jenice was her only kid. And that was when Aidan realised — it was the beginning of May, exactly a year ago today that it happened. How long does it take to get over losing someone and never knowing if she's still alive somewhere? More than a year, it seemed, judging from the crumpled-up expression on Mrs Trengove's face. And she seemed smaller, with a hunted sort of droop to her shoulders, like their border collie Bridie when Aidan's mum took her pups to the pet shop.

It made Aidan ask his mum some questions when he got home. 'Do you think there's another dimension somewhere?' He was careful how he said the next bit. 'Like — fairyland?'

Aidan's mother turned to look at him, a crease between her eyes. He thought he'd better explain some more. 'You know, some place where people might be when you think they're lost.' The crease on his mother's forehead forked down right into her eyes and turned watery. So she remembered Jenice too.

She came closer and put her hand on his head. 'So how do you feel, Aidan?'

'I saw Mrs Trengove in the shops. She's still sad.'

'I know. I'd feel awful if it happened to you.'

'Are you sure there's nothing across the creek?'

'Aidan, the police have been all over there. Every square centimetre. Down all the mine shafts — everywhere.'

'Maybe older people can't see it … you know, piskeys and stuff.' Aidan's voice trailed off as he saw the look in his mother's eyes. Not just sadness for Mrs Trengove and Jenice, but sadness for him now too. She put both arms around him.

'Please don't start thinking things like that, Aidan. Piskeys were just fairies, little trouble-makers in old stories people told to explain things too difficult to understand. Jenice's disappearance is something that's hard for us, but difficult things happen in life sometimes. We remember the people we loved, but we have to look forward to the next good thing too.'

And it was right then that Aidan could clearly hear Raff's voice in his head. He was sure of it. That singsong watery sound, and instantly Aidan knew what he had to do.

# Four

School next day was hard to sit through once
Aidan had decided on a plan of action. He didn't
think it would take long to go quickly across
the creek, keep out of the monster's way this time
and to check for any sign of Jenice. Then he
could come back for help. He didn't even tell
Josh, and he felt worse not telling his mum but
he knew she wouldn't believe what he'd seen,
and he'd only be gone half an hour. She'd think

he was at footy practice. Today he just wouldn't go.

'See ya then,' Josh called. 'You sure you're OK?'

'Yep.' Aidan grinned. Josh couldn't imagine anyone missing out on after-school footy practice. That was when you got picked for the school team. 'See you tomorrow.' Aidan ran to dump his bag over the stone wall of his garden. But first he took his muesli bar out and slipped it into his jeans pocket. Just then Bridie trotted round from the back; she always knew when he was going out.

'Bridie, I'm sorry, you can't come this time. I'll be back soon. Here, you mind my bag.' Aidan strode down the gravel track to the mine. He didn't look back once, even though he could hear Bridie's whining. Maybe now he could find out what happened to Jenice.

The closer he came to the creek and the stepping-stones the louder Raff's voice seemed. It made Aidan forget how scary it might be and when he reached the last stone, the piskey was already there.

He flew onto Aidan's shoulder and settled

with a happy whirr of wings. 'I knew you'd be coming back, boy.' And he laughed. 'Happy as a duck I be now. Come on. There be so much to show you.' Then he added, 'And so much to do. To do.'

'Do?'

But Raff only gave a chuckle for an answer, and directed Aidan further into the scrub, to an old mine shaft; he twisted his head to watch every way at once. Aidan respected Raff's carefulness; he didn't want to run into the dragaroo again.

'There be someone you must be meeting,' Raff said as Aidan began to climb down wooden rungs into the hole. Aidan saw the walls, scraped where people had dug and picked at them for years. 'She's been waiting.'

'She? Who?' Aidan's words swooped back at him again and again like an owl's call, then hovered in the air, but Raff didn't explain. Soon they reached the bottom and a tunnel opened in front of them as if welcoming them in.

'Do you think this is a good idea?' Aidan asked, squinting to see in the faint light from the circle of sky above.

'It may be as dark as your hat down here, but 'tis the path to our land, boy.' That was when Aidan first heard the music — it was a living thing breathing around him, curling up to him. He could swear if he reached out, he could pat it, even though he couldn't see it. The sound was like the flutes he heard in the school music room, only he never felt like this when he heard them. This sound had fingers and was gently pulling him. It made him want to press closer, to hear it better. Raff chuckled in Aidan's ear. 'No need to fear, boy. The Lady it be — calling you.'

First they descended a few more steps, and then passages spread in all directions just as Aidan imagined they would in an underground mine. He was surprised to find how much light shone from the glistening walls.

'This way,' Raff said, directing, when Aidan stood between two archways. But it was the music that truly led them, and the further underground they went, the stronger the music grew.

'Here,' Aidan said. Three passageways yawned in front of them. Aidan never liked to dilly around, even when he felt nervous — he may as well try one, so he turned to the right. Instantly, the music swirled around him, pushing him back. He could feel it as strongly as a hot north wind.

'Left, boy,' Raff urged with his usual chuckle, and a pull on Aidan's ear. 'This way.'

At the next meeting of passageways, Aidan hesitated. He didn't want to turn the wrong way, but could he feel the music's direction before Raff told him? 'Shh,' he said as he felt Raff stirring. And maybe that was how he heard the knocking above the tune.

'What's that?'

'What's what?' Raff's laugh died away. 'Just follow the music, boy.'

'Knocking. It sounds like someone working in here. With a pick.'

Raff relaxed, but only slightly. 'That be the knockers, boy. They still work the mine.'

'There are people down here?' Aidan shut his ears to the music and stepped into the passageway.

'No, boy, the music. Be you deaf as a haddock, boy? Listen to the music.' And suddenly the music was swirling around Aidan like a whirly wind. He couldn't hear the knocking any more but to the side he thought he glimpsed a shadow. Then it was gone.

'Back up, boy,' Raff urged. He put one skinny arm around Aidan's neck. 'The music always keeps us safe.' Raff didn't sound so confident now, and suddenly the shape was there — in front of them — smaller than a dwarf. And just as quickly it disappeared. Aidan heard laughing, higher pitched than Raff's, and he sensed that familiar shiver in his middle. The face he fleetingly saw reminded him of his mother's garden gnome, only this one was wrinkled and pale with huge white eyes.

'Oh, we've upset them now, boy. We'll be having terrible bad luck — they'll never let us pass again, unless …'

'Unless what?' Aidan asked even though he wasn't sure he believed in luck at all.

'Very easily put out, they be. They like to be helped. Food. You wouldn't be having any food in your pocket?'

'How about a muesli bar?'

'As long as 'tis edible. Leave it on the ground, boy. On the ground.'

Aidan unwrapped the bar and did as Raff said, then he backed out of the tunnel onto the main passageway. The laughing behind them changed tone.

'A relief 'tis, boy. We'll be right as ninepence now. They like your food and will always let you pass. Just be following the music now. Please?'

Aidan grinned at the 'please'. Raff was treating him as though he was an important visitor and Aidan couldn't work out why. Hadn't he himself decided to come? And surely Raff could just zap him into doing the right thing? Why did he give Aidan a choice in the tunnel?

The music was louder than ever now they were in the main passage. There were places Aidan had to duck his head to get through, but now the ground began to rise. It seemed lighter too, and suddenly in front of them was a wall with ledges cut into it and a rope either side to hang onto.

'This be it,' Raff said, lifting off from Aidan's shoulder. 'See those steps? Up you go.'

'What about you?'

'I'll be behind you. 'Tis you the Lady be waiting to see.'

What if there was a dragaroo up there? But this time Aidan had no choice for the music floated around him and tugged at him even more effectively than Raff's words could have done. Up Aidan climbed.

# Five

Aidan hauled himself up the steps — there must have been a hundred. He lost count. Imagine being a miner and doing this every morning and night. No thanks. At least the music sounded encouraging — half of him wanted to get out to see where it came from, the other half was uneasy. What would be out there?

When he finally dragged himself over the top ledge, he lay on the step, panting and looking out, his eyes wide, his mouth open. It was a green lake — the colour of the stones that lay near the mine shafts. It was almost as big as an inland sea, metallic and sparkly, shifting slightly in the muted sunlight. On the far side there were cliffs — lime, lilac and ochre. They looked as if they'd been coloured in with pastel chalks. Pink and white clay stretched as far as he could see and the leaves on the trees and bushes were purple and green, and shone as if they were sprayed with iridescent paint. The air smelt like flowers and fruit — mango, no — lemon, or was it pineapple? Aidan wasn't sure. And there by the water, not far from Aidan, stood Raff's Lady.

She didn't look fierce or dangerous; her dress was as blue as peacock feathers and it floated in the breeze. Her dark hair hung to her shoulders. She was small, as high as Aidan's knee, and she hadn't been playing a flute — it was a tin whistle. Aidan wondered how she was able to play such hypnotic music. She had a welcoming smile but Aidan had the feeling she was used to telling people what to do.

'Come closer, Aidan Curnow. Welcome to

Trevalia. We have been waiting.' Her voice was like water, silvery and splashy. Aidan stood and she stepped aside. At the water's edge he saw a little wooden boat with a boy in it even smaller than the Lady. His hands were on the paddles.

'Come.'

Aidan checked behind him. Sure enough there was Raff and he flew onto Aidan's shoulder as Aidan walked towards the boat. How would he fit inside?

The Lady kept beckoning to him and, just as Aidan put his foot inside, the boat was suddenly bigger, roomy enough for them all to sit down. There were so many questions Aidan wanted to ask. Why was the boat bigger inside than out? Had he shrunk? But the Lady was still small and Raff fitted on his shoulder as before. Why was the Lady waiting for him? And why hadn't anyone in town heard about this place across the creek? The Lady called it Trevalia.

'Never fear, Aidan. All your questions will be answered.'

Aidan pulled his head up in shock. The Lady knew what he'd been thinking. She was smiling at him, showing him where they were headed — a hole in one of the cliffs. Aidan shivered. The hole looked like a cave that you could get trapped in forever. To calm himself Aidan stared out at the green water, watched the wash build up beside them as the small boy rowed.

Suddenly, just beyond the waves made by the oars, Aidan saw a ripple. Just the sort you see when fish are under the surface nibbling at bread you've thrown in, but this ripple was bigger than fish bubbles, more like a whale's. The ripple followed the boat — a circle of bubbles to one side, then the other. Aidan glanced at the Lady. She was smiling, staring out across the lake. She hadn't noticed anything at all. And he didn't feel like asking Raff in case he got flustered and upset the boat — then they'd be in the water with whatever was down there.

The Lady was smiling at Aidan when next he glanced at her and strangely his quivers fell away; he felt safe as though there was nothing to be con-cerned about at all. They soon beached on the other side and he helped the small boy rope the boat to a wooden post. It was a tricky task with

Raff hanging on around his neck. Whenever Aidan bent down, Raff swung around to Aidan's back, but sometimes the piskey was caught unawares and was left dangling.

Aidan looked out to the lake again, but there wasn't a ripple in sight. He turned back to the small boy — maybe he knew what the ripple was — and that was when Aidan noticed the boy's ears. They were pointed like an actor's on *Star Trek*, except that these were real. There wasn't time to ask about it for the Lady led Aidan through a well-tended garden into the hole in the hill, down stone steps, like a staircase, then along a passage, not as long as the one in the mine. Suddenly he could hear more music — a tin whistle, harps, bells, all blended into one high happy sound.

He turned a corner, and stood staring down at a party. He was in a cave that had been mined out of the earth and rock. The walls were covered in green, blue and purple ore that sparkled as if it were aflame. And the beams weren't made of wood but of quartz. That wasn't all. Just like the Lady, the guests were small people, with ears like the boat boy, and piskeys like Raff were dancing in the air and singing. A lot of the small men wore green clothes with sky-blue jackets and three-cornered hats, but the small ladies wore long dresses that made them look like a garden of flowers. The dresses had lace and silver bells that tinkled as the ladies danced. The dancing piskeys hung like a rainbow in the air. The Lady clapped her hands and the music and tinkling stopped.

'He is come,' was all she said. There was a cheer and immediately the dancing and music continued.

She turned to Aidan. 'They are welcoming you; they have waited a long time.' Aidan didn't think it had been long since he saw the dragaroo — two days actually, but he decided not to argue with the Lady and he followed her down to a great stone table set with fruit and pies, and sweets coloured like a sea of Smarties.

The Lady clapped her hands again and the piskeys flew to the table to join the feast, hovering over the dishes like giant, colourful dragonflies. Aidan sat where Raff directed, next to the Lady. Raff kept flying to the middle of the table to fetch Aidan different kinds of fruit. Most of it Aidan had never seen before — berries that looked like purple blackberries and grapes that were blue.

'Have some fairy bread,' Raff offered. Aidan was about to say no — he didn't feel like hundreds and thousands on buttered bread. But when he saw what Raff held he took it — it was the colour of raw sugar and it smelt spicy. ''Tis fruit rolled into bread.'

Aidan swallowed — it tasted a heap better than it sounded. Even the bread was so airy it almost floated away before it melted on his tongue.

'What be the best thing to put your teeth into?' Raff asked, grinning.

'What?' By the look on Raff's face, Aidan knew a joke was coming.

'Fairy bread, of course.' Laughing, Raff flew off to get Aidan another piece. Aidan didn't laugh. Piskeys sure told weak jokes. After more fairy bread, he thought lollies would never taste so good again. Even the small people's chocolate dissolved in his mouth and it wasn't even brown — it took the colour of whatever fruit it was made from.

Suddenly, Aidan sensed the Lady watching

him. He looked up. It was strange — he didn't feel in any danger at all, even though it seemed he was in a dream, and everyone knows how unpredictable dreams are. Surely he was too wide-awake for this to be a dream?

The Lady smiled. 'We have some children in our land … Children like you,' she added, for Aidan was looking at the boy who rowed the boat. 'Human children.'

Aidan felt a sudden flying feeling in his chest. *Jenice*. 'Is Jenice Trengove here?'

'She was.' And the Lady sighed. 'But she has been taken, along with the others, to the Dark Bush.' She hesitated before saying any more and stared intently at him. It made Aidan stop chewing. The music seemed to grow softer.

'Aidan Curnow, we need you to bring them back.'

# Six

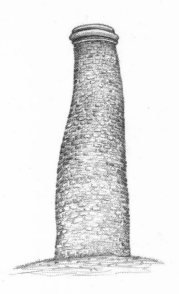

'Me?' Aidan looked hard at the Lady; all the small people and piskeys were listening now too. Surely a Lady who lived in a land across the creek with hundreds of piskeys that flew could do anything at all even if she was small. So he blurted it out, hoping he didn't sound rude. 'Why don't you?'

She smiled. 'Only a human who has walked across the water can be free to overcome the ones that have taken the children captive.'

Aidan didn't feel hungry anymore. 'You mean they're fierce like the dragaroo?'

The Lady sighed. 'The dragaroo is their pet. They bred it.' She said this as though they didn't do a very good job of it. 'They are the spriggans, warrior fairies. They steal children — sometimes even from your land. They bring storms and torment anything in their path.'

'And you want me to rescue the kids from them? Why me?'

The music stopped altogether as the Lady answered. 'No one else has crossed the water and survived a dragaroo attack. No one else has been brave enough to return a second time.'

The Lady leant closer to Aidan. 'Do not worry, for Raff will go with you.'

Aidan felt like saying, 'Big deal.' But when the Lady smiled, Aidan bit his lip — he remembered that she understood his thoughts.

'And you may take the whistle — it will be more help than you think.'

'Besides,' Raff added, 'you have eaten magic food —'twill be giving you extraordinary strength.'

Aidan didn't think he was brave. Maybe he

should tell them. Nor did he feel any different — just that he couldn't wait to find Jenice.

'And, Aidan Curnow, this you must remember well,' the Lady said. 'If, at any time, you are in danger from the spriggans you must turn your coat inside out.'

Aidan tried hard not to let himself think how weird that was. How could changing your coat around help?

'So where is this Dark Bush?' he asked instead. He might as well get on with it. Wasn't this why he came?

The Lady smiled. 'I knew you wouldn't disappoint us. The Dark Bush is on the east side of Trevalia, across the Green Lake. Raff will show you the way.'

# Seven

The Lady said Aidan could take the boat but the boy with the pointed ears was nowhere to be seen. Aidan was glad he had done some rowing on the creek before the danger signs went up last year. Though right now rowing wasn't Aidan's greatest concern. He glanced at Raff sitting there in the stern of the boat. He looked like a little sergeant-major ready to give orders.

'Do you think the lake is safe, Raff?'

For a split second Aidan caught a strange look on Raff's face as though he was about to tell a joke, but was deciding against it.

'Of course. Don't be worrying. The Lady wouldn't ask you to go if she didn't think you could manage.'

'I'll never give up until I find Jenice.'

'Good. We be happy as ducks then.'

Aidan wasn't sure if Raff gave helpful advice for didn't his mother say piskeys were trouble-makers? But why would the Lady let Raff go with him if he was a troublemaker? And what if the Lady didn't know everything, as she seemed to? What if she didn't know there was something making ripples in the lake?

Aidan shrugged and got into the boat. Whatever it was it couldn't be as bad as the draga-roo. That would have surfaced by now if it was in the lake, wouldn't it? Aidan set the oars in the rowlocks and pulled. Soon they were in the middle of the water. Raff had just begun to sing when Aidan noticed the ripples again.

*'Rainbow at morn, put your hook in the corn.'*

The ripples appeared on Aidan's left side, not too close, then they followed the boat.

*'Rainbow at eve, put your head in the sheave.'*

Aidan tried to relax. If it was dangerous Raff would be flapping — he seemed to be a thermometer for danger. It must be okay — though Aidan couldn't help wondering what Raff was about to say before he got into the boat with him. Then, just as silently as they came, the ripples disappeared. Aidan searched all around the boat. He couldn't see one anywhere. As he turned back he caught Raff staring at him, grinning. 'Everything all right, boy?'

Annoyed, Aidan said, 'Sure.' It wasn't long before they reached the other side and Aidan dragged the boat up onto the coloured pebbles. They stood on another part of the lake shore now where a field of flowers grew, like a red and purple carpet. The Lady's orchard was close by. Aidan picked a plum — it was as big as an orange and tasted better than any fruit he'd bought from a shop.

Raff directed Aidan to the east. 'The land of

the Dark Bush is this way.' Aidan couldn't see it yet. Strangely this mine area had become a whole lot bigger than he remembered.

Just as Aidan's legs began to get tired another orchard loomed into view. Raff flew ahead — checking for danger, he said. 'Don't eat anything here,' he called as he soared off. Aidan couldn't believe the number of different fruit trees. So many colours and shapes. He was sure the fruit would taste brilliant too. He reached up and picked a piece that looked like a bright pink peach except the skin wasn't furry. Surely this wasn't what Raff meant. Aidan was just about to bite into it when Raff dived in like a jet bomber. 'No. No! Don't eat it!'

In fright, Aidan dropped it. 'What's wrong? It's just fruit.'

''Tis not "just fruit".' Raff was hovering right in front of Aidan's face. It made Aidan cross-eyed to look at him.

'It looks like the fruit at your feast, and in that other orchard.'

'But 'tisn't *our* fruit — 'tis the spriggans'.'

Aidan couldn't tell the difference and most

probably Jenice and the other children couldn't either. 'If you eat it —' Raff lowered his voice and Aidan had to lean closer, so that Raff's wings beat on his nose, '— they be catching you.' Raff made it sound the most horrible thing possible, and that was where Jenice was now. With these spriggans.

'We'd better get a move on then,' Aidan said, though as he began tramping again he wondered how many more traps there would be before they found Jenice and the kids.

# Eight

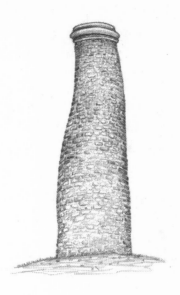

'We be getting closer,' Raff said. 'There 'tis — the land of the Dark Bush.'

The Dark Bush made Aidan shiver as if the sun had already set. It was dusky and full of half-grown, twisted gums and gnarled bushes. And they weren't in shiny colours like the leaves in the Lady's land. Some were dull grey and others even looked brownish-black. Through them Aidan could see lights swaying, as though they were dancing lanterns: ochre, yellow and orange. They looked like the phosphorescent flashes he'd seen in the sea one night with his dad. 'Let's check them out.' Aidan moved closer to see them better. 'Maybe they'll show the way.' His mum had told him a story about that once. A boy got lost and followed the lights of glow-worms home.

'No! They be jack-o'-lanterns, boy. That's how the spriggans be luring children.'

But Aidan didn't stop. He kept walking towards the lights, watching them as though he couldn't take his gaze away. They were flickering like the stars on his ceiling at home. 'They don't look so bad.'

Raff flapped around his head like a bird distracting a cat too close to her nest.

''Tis what they hope you'll be thinking. People follow them, never to be seen again.'

It didn't work — Aidan was drawing closer to the lights now. Raff tried harder. 'You'll never be seeing Jenice again, if you keep walking that way. Spriggan spit! You'll never be rescuing her.'

Aidan shuddered. Suddenly he paused. *Jenice*. Of course. He shook his head to clear it. Imagine if he didn't have Raff with him. He'd be spriggan supper. 'I'm sorry. It was like I didn't know what I was doing.'

'I know,' Raff said. 'That be how it works. 'Tis this way now.'

They turned back, carried on up a hill, past more 'Danger' signs, until suddenly a mine chimney loomed up out of the darkness.

''Tis the entrance to their underworld,' Raff announced.

'Isn't there a back way?' Aidan stared at the gaping hole near the bottom of the chimney.

'Any way we go in they will be knowing.'

'So how do we get in without them attacking?'

'The music, boy.' Aidan relaxed as he remembered the whistle in his pocket. The Lady said it would help. 'But you must be playing for it to work,' Raff said.

'Why?'

'Use your noggin, boy. My fingers don't reach the holes for a start. Besides the Lady said 'twas for you to do.'

'Me? Kids at school say my recorder playing is

like a sick crow.' Actually they said a lot of ruder things than that but Aidan wasn't sure Raff would understand.

Raff shrugged as he pulled the whistle from Aidan's pocket, flew up and held it out. 'Are you brave enough or are you a duck — more gab than guts?'

Aidan grinned. Maybe Raff would understand the words his friends said. He took the whistle and put it to his lips, blew into it and moved his fingers a bit. The holes were closer together than on a recorder and to his surprise a sound came out not unlike the Lady's. Encouraged, he kept moving his fingers while Raff on his shoulder pointed out where to step. Aidan didn't feel as though he was the one making the music at all, yet when he moved his fingers, the haunting music played. He slipped down into the darkness, his fingers on the whistle. He wondered how they'd see — the tunnel was darker than the entrance to the Lady's land — but Raff had a dancing light of his own. He held it in his hand like a candle flame while Aidan tried not to be nervous of the shadows it caused.

At the first passageway that veered off to the left, Aidan paused, but Raff waved him on. 'Don't stop. Don't stop. The music will be showing us.'

In the next passage a stone fell from the roof. Aidan jumped and for an instant broke off his playing.

'Keep playing!' Raff snapped. It seemed his grins and jokes had disappeared with the light.

After three more passageways that Raff said to ignore, the music changed tone slightly and he finally pointed to the right. Here was a small cave of plain rock with sharp ledges, not sparkly like the Lady's cavern. They crept in, Raff's hand-light showed the way. There were shapes on the floor. Many of them. Aidan stood there, staring. This time he stopped playing altogether.

# Nine

In the dim light Aidan could see shapes on the ground — humps, as though bodies were strewn there. Was he too late? Then he heard a moan.

'Jenice? Is that you?'

'Who is it?' That sounded like Jenice. There was a rustle from a girl beside her.

Aidan stepped forward. Jenice didn't sit up to greet him — maybe she was sick.

'It's Aidan Curnow.' Then he could see her face.

She still looked the same, even though she was lying down. With her were other children, some in strange clothes. One had on a dress with a white apron over the top. There was even a girl in a swimsuit and a boy with only a possum skin around his waist. Aidan wondered if they ever felt cold. Was there winter in this land? One boy was wearing woollen shorts and long socks. Aidan had only seen clothes like that in his school history book.

'Jenice!' He knelt down. The kids' clothes weren't the only odd thing. He suddenly realised why they were all on the ground. 'You're tied up. What is this mucky stuff?' Aidan reached out. What he touched made him think of sticky, stringy bubble gum and giant spiders. 'Gross. Cobwebs?'

'They're magic cobwebs,' Jenice said. 'And they're strong as fishing line. We've tried but we can't break them.'

'The music, boy,' Raff prompted in Aidan's ear. Aidan began to play again, and as he did so, Jenice strained against the webs and broke free. She then began pulling webs from the smaller kids. He had a flash in his mind of her helping him up onto the cubby roof. Funny how she didn't look any older. Aidan was bigger than her now, but he was sure he wasn't last year.

Jenice couldn't believe it was Aidan. When all the kids were free of the webs, she asked, 'So you fell in the creek too?'

'No, I walked across the stones.' He looked behind him. 'Haven't seen any spriggans.' He said it as if he didn't believe they were real and Jenice looked sharply at him.

'You will. I think they're going to eat us. This cave is their pantry.'

Aidan looked around and saw what she meant — there were bones scattered in all the corners. 'Messy, aren't they?'

Raff was fidgety on Aidan's shoulder. 'Stop chittering like a flock of magpies. We have to be going, boy. Get the children together. The music — 'tis not good to stop.'

Jenice agreed with Raff, Aidan could tell by her half-smile and the way she kept glancing at the little kids, but he wanted to know more. 'So you've been in Trevalia all this time?'

She frowned as if she had never thought of that before. 'I've only been here a few weeks, I think.' She brushed down her jeans and gathered the kids closer. There were eight of them and she was the biggest. 'We were collecting fruit for the Lady when we followed some lights and those horrible spriggans found us. Some kids, like Josie here, have been with the Lady for years. This is Will — he's been here for years too,' and the boy with the woollen shorts grinned at Aidan. More like centuries, Aidan thought, as he watched Josie set straight a little girl's white hat that reminded him of his mum's shower cap.

'Actually you've been gone a year, Jenice. A year yesterday.'

She turned a horrified face to Aidan. 'A *year*! You're kidding.' But she could see he wasn't. 'So it happened to me too. Mum will be frantic.' Aidan wasn't sure what 'it' was but he didn't get to ask, nor did he tell her they'd had a remembrance service and there was a special drinking fountain at school with her name on it.

'We have to be going!' Raff poked Aidan in the ear. 'Play, boy. Play!'

They were standing at the entrance of the cave and that was when they heard the rushing sound. Aidan thought it sounded like a runaway train in a tunnel. Raff started to shake and flutter on Aidan's shoulder. ''Tis them,' he moaned. 'Spriggan spit! 'Tis too late. Too late.'

'Never too late,' Aidan muttered, and he started playing the whistle. Jenice asked Josie and Will to take the other children down the passage to the chimney entrance, then she lifted up the little girl with the cap and stayed beside Aidan as he walked backwards at the end of the line. When he saw the first spriggan he almost tripped, and he stopped playing for more than a second.

'Play!' Raff screamed, for that moment gave the spriggans an advantage — they sprang up closer, as if daring the music to hurt them. They were small like Raff but Aidan thought they looked as if they could make a nasty gash in his leg. Then Aidan had a horrible thought — what if the music didn't work? Without any reason, the spriggans came even closer. He could see into the eyes of the leader. Any horror stories he'd read didn't prepare him for how ugly it was. Worse than trolls or hyenas. These spriggans were grey like the cobwebs and they drooled yellow slime.

Their eyes were bloodshot and their teeth were long and sharp. Aidan was sure they had dog's breath. It was obvious they ate meat for dinner and suddenly Aidan was determined not to be on the menu. He played faster. Of course the music will work. Didn't the Lady say so?

Just as they scrambled through the chimney opening, Aidan shouted, 'Run for it!' He kept on playing so the spriggans wouldn't catch them but suddenly the leader started groaning and its body looked as if it was straining to burst out of its skin.

'What's it doing?' Jenice asked, so horrified she stopped to stare.

Raff answered her in a wail. 'Spriggans can change their size when they wish.' And he started moaning.

Aidan didn't dare stop playing, for while he played the spriggans were wary and kept their distance, but just then the giant spriggan, as big as Aidan now, picked up a stone and threw it at him. It landed too close, close enough to startle him and make him drop the whistle which rolled away between two rocks behind him. He dived as if he was marking a footy, but he couldn't reach it.

'The whistle! Too deep. Too deep.' Raff was in the air, flapping and going nowhere. Aidan knew there'd be no point running now. If the spriggans could change their size their steps would be so much bigger. Now there were more of them pouring out from under the chimney, like unsure ants from a disturbed anthill, small and disorganised, but what if they all grew and charged at once? There was only one thing to do.

'Keep the kids behind me, Jenice, there's something I have to try.'

'What can you do? Your hand's too big to get the whistle out.'

'Something the Lady told me.' Aidan hurriedly unzipped his coat.

Raff was frantic. 'No time. No time. Run. Run as fast as you can. They be coming.' He flew onto Jenice's shoulder — she was further away.

Aidan tugged one arm out of its sleeve. Now for the second. Why did something so simple take so long! He tried walking backwards to gain more time but he was not quick enough.

# Ten

'Ow!' Something was pricking him, tripping him, and suddenly he fell. The small spriggans swarmed over him like bees. Aidan felt like an echidna with its quills shoved in the wrong way.

'Get off!' He tried to push himself up. Surely he could knock off the little brutes so long as they stayed small, but he couldn't move. His hair was held down to the ground and all he could see was sticky grey cobwebs in front of his eyes. The spriggans gathered round him on the ground, jumping up and down, even the big one, their mouths leering at him while he struggled to break free.

'Aidan!' It was Jenice. Her voice came closer.

The spriggans would get her too, unless she could do in time what the Lady had said. 'Jenice, turn your coat inside out!'

'You crazy? How will that help?'

The spriggans looked up with a single grunt as she spoke.

'Do it!'

Just then the giant spriggan crouched, ready to spring.

'Quick!'

Jenice didn't hesitate; she pulled off her coat, fumbling as she tried to turn it inside out quickly. One of her hands stuck in a sleeve lining, she was trembling so much. Then she got the coat back on with all the seams poking out, just as the giant spriggan sprang towards her. It was about to catch hold of her when in mid-leap it saw the coat. Suddenly it howled and fell onto the ground beside her as if someone invisible had hit it in the face. Everyone watched wide-eyed as it shrank to its normal size. But it didn't stop there; it started to disappear. The other spriggans became smaller too until they were all gone. Even Aidan's cobwebs fell off in a limp mess on the ground.

'It's not the end of them, though,' Raff said, laughing again as he flew up to Aidan's shoulder. He settled there as the children stood grinning around Aidan and Jenice. Aidan couldn't believe how Raff could sound cheery again so soon. He was relieved too but he didn't feel like laughing. 'We'd better get out of the Dark Bush right now. Turning your coat only works the once.' That started the kids murmuring together.

'Look what I 'ave,' said Will in the woollen shorts. He held up the tin whistle. Her had a long, thin stick in his other hand.

Jenice hugged him while Aidan put the whistle in his pocket. 'You're so clever, Will. Let's take it back to the Lady.'

# Eleven

Raff didn't let them rest a second. 'Come on,' he said. 'We have to be away from spriggan land.'

Aidan didn't feel like asking why but he could imagine what Raff meant. Warrior fairies that could change their size wouldn't let their dinner go easily. 'They were seriously ugly.'

Raff agreed with a chuckle. 'Iss, yes, no one will be stopping their horse from galloping, to look at them, that be for sure.'

Raff flew off to see the way ahead, and shadows shifted in the Dark Bush. 'Let's keep the little ones close to us,' Aidan said, checking around him.

'Sure.' Jenice rearranged the line. 'Hedley can go on the end. Josie in the middle. Will, can you help with the younger ones near the front?'

'No one is to eat any fruit,' Aidan said as they came to the orchard.

'We know,' Jenice said. 'The Lady warned us.'

'Then how did you get caught by the spriggans?'

'The lights. The younger kids can't seem to resist them. I find it hard too.'

'I almost didn't either,' Aidan admitted. 'But I had Raff.'

'You came to Trevalia a different way from us. Are you sure you didn't fall in the creek?'

'No.'

'The rest of us did. Maybe that's why everything affects us more.'

'And why you stay maybe.'

'I've never thought of going home. It wasn't until I saw you that I remembered I should go home before Mum worries.'

Bit late for that, Aidan thought. 'So will you come home with me now?'

'I want to — I hope the Lady will let us go.'

'What do you mean? Of course she will.'

'The little kids were here before me. They say she loves us all.'

'Aye,' broke in Josie. 'She loves us too much to let us go.'

'You too, now,' Will said.

'But you said Jenice 'as been gone a year yes-terd'y,' Josie said. 'That's a year-and-a-day. My mam always said a year-and-a-day was a magic time. Jenice could leave if 'tis still a year-and-a-day when we go back to the Lady's cave.'

'And the Lady wouldn't be able to stop her?' Aidan asked.

Josie half shook her head. 'I don't think so.'

'But she'll try,' Will warned.

Aidan stared at Jenice. She shrugged and started counting the children. 'Nine. There are nine of us now.'

'Let's hurry,' Aidan said then. 'Before the time is up. The sooner we get back to the cave the sooner we will find out if we can get away.'

# Twelve

Aidan and Jenice led the children through the spriggans' orchard. 'No eating anything,' Jenice reminded everyone.

'I'm hungry,' said the smallest boy. Aidan noticed his old-fashioned canvas sneakers. Jenice lifted him up. 'Come on, Steven. We have to walk faster.'

'Iss, faster, faster,' Raff said, flying back from the trees. He settled on Aidan's shoulder.

'The spriggans could come again.' That started the little girl whimpering. Raff flew off again. 'Be back dreckly, need to check for shadows. Shadows.'

'I hope Raff won't be scouting for long,' Aidan said to Jenice. 'He might be small but I feel safer when he's around.'

Then Will said something odd. 'You shouldn't put too much faith in Raff. You must be remembering he belongs to the Lady's land.'

'What's that got to do with anything?' Aidan asked, but no one heard him for the whimpering girl put her hands up to Jenice. Jenice shook her head; her arms were full with Steven.

'Like a piggy back?' Aidan asked and he knelt down while the little girl climbed on. 'What's your name?'

'Molly.' Molly was the one in the funny hat whom Aidan had first noticed in the cave; now her dress and petticoat hung down to Aidan's knees. He had to be careful not to get his hand caught in the material when he checked that the whistle was in his pocket.

'So where did you live before you came here?'

'At the mine,' Molly said.

'In the mine?' Aidan thought she must be too young to know her real address. There were no houses in the mine. He glanced over at Jenice to check.

She nodded. 'Josie said Molly lived in one of the cottages that were at the mine.'

'But that was years ago. A century even!'

'More.'

'This is weird, Jenice. What about you, Will? Where did you live?'

'In Lucas Street. My Da works in the mine too — he's a smelter. We was coming all the way from Wales in a boat with three grand sails.'

Aidan stared at Will. So that explained his long woollen shorts and long braces and funny shirt with the round collar. 'The mine isn't working any more,' Aidan said carefully. 'Did you know that?'

Will didn't answer and Jenice switched Steven to her other hip. 'I tried explaining to them when I came, but it's best to leave it alone.' She leant closer to Aidan and whispered, 'Josie and Will suspect they are all from different times but even they don't really understand that their world is in the past, and it would upset them if they did. Imagine telling them their parents are all dead, their houses and everything they knew gone.'

Aidan stared at her in horror. 'They don't know?'

Jenice shook her head. 'They don't seem to understand what happened. And I don't think the Lady ever explained it to them.'

'So some of them have been here over a hundred years?'

Jenice looked behind her. 'See the Aboriginal boy?'

Aidan nodded.

'He'd never heard a word of English before he came to Trevalia … So how long do you think he's been here, Aidan?'

Aiden looked thoughtfully at the boy.

'Since the time the mine got underway, I guess, since the Lady came with the first Cornish folk. Mr Penna said in social studies the mine started in 1844.'

So long ago … 160 years. Aidan took another

look at the Aboriginal boy. He had the possum skin tucked around his waist. Didn't his chest get cold? 'What's his name?'

'Warretya, but he told Will to call him Warrie.'

'Will understood him?'

'Will had a friend like Warrie, before he fell in the creek. They used to play together near the mine.' Then Jenice sighed. 'I didn't realise it was the same for me — a whole year.'

'And a day.'

Jenice looked up at Aidan. 'You're different now. You were smaller than me and I used to tell you what to do.'

'I think I'm older than you now, by half a year. You haven't grown here at all. Look at the kids — they've been here for years but they must be the same as when they first came.'

'I know — I guess that's why it's called Trevalia — fairyland. Is Mum okay?'

'She's sad.' This was the first time Aidan dared say it. 'She thinks you're dead. Everyone does.'

Jenice stopped walking. 'Dead? That's dreadful.'

'A year's a long time.'

Just then Raff flew in and landed on Molly's back. She giggled, but Raff wasn't laughing. Aidan braced himself for trouble — Raff was fluttering and flapping. Something had to be wrong. 'Come on, come on. You be all so slow you be going sideways like a crab to jail. There be shadows lurking, lurking in the Dark Bush — they be shifting.'

'When will it get lighter?' Aidan asked, not liking the sound of shifting shadows. And didn't the orchard seem bigger than when he and Raff first came?

'Only when we be away from the Dark Bush. That's why it has its name, boy — 'tis dark, dark as a dog's guts. The spriggans don't like the light of the Lady's land.'

Jenice turned to check the children. She counted them. 'Eight. Where's Hedley?'

Aidan stopped. 'One's missing? Did we leave him in the cave?' He frowned. He felt the familiar quivers in his middle as if a centipede was in there starting to bite; he certainly didn't feel like going back now — but if he had to …

'No, I counted them at the start of the

spriggans' orchard.' Then Jenice looked at Raff. 'Could you fly up please and see if he's close by?'

Raff did so, his wings buzzing as he hovered. 'Iss! I see him. Oh, spriggan spit!'

'What is it?' Both Aidan and Jenice shouted at once.

'He be walking towards the jack-o'-lanterns!'

Jenice groaned. 'That's how the spriggans caught us in the first place. I shouldn't have left him at the back — but I thought he'd be all right. He's as sensible as Will.'

'No one be sensible when it comes to jack-o'-lanterns,' Raff said.

'I'll get him.' Aidan handed Molly to Will. 'You keep the kids moving through the orchard, Jenice.'

Raff directed Aidan through the orchard, flying above his head and giving directions. 'No, this way, boy. Are you daff? Not south-west, north-east.' He sounded so ruffled and Aidan thought Raff should have more sympathy; it was hard to see ahead in an orchard of huge trees when the light was dim and you couldn't fly.

Soon Aidan could see the child. 'Hedley!'

'He won't hear you, boy. You have to catch him.'

'Why?'

'The jack-o'-lanterns have caught his eyes, his mind. 'Tis all he can see or hear. Catch him before he reaches the lights.' And Raff flew down and hung on to Aidan's neck as Aidan ran.

Soon Aidan could see them — the dancing lights, hear high-pitched laughter. The lights were kind of pretty. Flickering like lights on a harbour in the summer. They reminded him of holidays he had with his parents at Moonta Bay — a jetty and boats and fishing at night.

'Boy! Concentrate!' Raff perched right on top of Aidan's head, hung down and covered Aidan's eyes with his little hands. The dark coolness woke Aidan up.

'Whew, those lights are powerful.'

'That they be. Now don't be looking at them. Just be catching the young one.'

Hedley was steadily marching towards the lights, not running. It was as if he was a remote control car and the lights were guiding him home. Except it wouldn't be home for Hedley. Aidan shuddered — it would be the spriggans' pantry cave. Aidan ran faster. Just as he reached Hedley he was aware of a shadow to the side. Then another in front.

'Quickly!' Raff screamed, almost falling off Aidan's shoulder in fright.

Aidan reached Hedley and clung to his shoulder, tried to turn him. It didn't work.

'His eyes, boy,' Raff shouted. 'His eyes.'

Aidan covered Hedley's eyes with his hands and almost immediately the boy faltered, then stopped. 'Come on,' Aidan said, turning him so he couldn't see the lights. 'We have to get out of here.'

Just then Aidan felt a nip on his ankle, sensed the wind of something flitting past him. Then he saw a pair of eyes — red and bloodshot, and he was aware of a string of slime on his hand, imagined a set of pointed yellow teeth sunk into his leg. The spriggans. They were there already!

'The whistle, boy!'

It was almost too late but Aidan managed to get it out of his jeans pocket and start playing. The spriggans fell back, but they circled the boys.

Aidan tried not to dwell on how hungry and mean they looked. He kept the shaking Hedley under one arm while he played. Raff added instructions from the air. 'Louder. Faster. To the left.' Aidan thought Raff sounded like the director of a horror movie. He tried to run as fast as he could while still playing and trying not to trip over Hedley. He couldn't even pause to comfort the poor boy who was crying now and making Aidan's coat damp.

Raff flew ahead to warn Jenice. Aidan could even hear him shouting above the sound of the whistle. For a delicate little thing with wings, Raff had a big voice. 'You must wait for the music or the spriggans will surely be catching someone. Here be Aidan. Finally.' Raff sounded as if Aidan had been strolling, not crashing through the orchard pursued by ugly little spriggans.

When Aidan reached Jenice she took Hedley's hand. 'Hang on, Steven,' she cried to the boy on her hip.

This time Aidan managed to run faster and to play at the same time. Raff flew above, moaning and shouting by turns. 'The directions be terrible mixed up. I don't know this way. 'Tis not the way we came. We'll be lost.'

Aidan didn't care, so long as they got out of the horrible Dark Bush. Anything would have to be better than being eaten alive by slimy spriggans.

# Thirteen

Soon the trees started to thin out. 'It's getting brighter,' Jenice cried. 'We'll be okay now. The spriggans don't like daylight.'

Aidan checked behind him. There was nothing there other than the dark tunnels between the trees. No horrible pale spriggans with gaping mouths and slimy drool. Ahead, he could see the sunlight glinting on the green leaves and he stopped playing the whistle. At that everybody stopped running. Will and Jenice were puffed out from carrying Molly and Steven. They put the little ones down and walked slowly into the sunshine, sucking in rasping breaths. Aidan found his side hurt and his chest did too when he breathed out.

'Let's sit here,' Jenice suggested. She pointed to a shaded area with a huge rock hanging over it.

'I'm not liking it, not liking it,' Raff said. Aidan thought he sounded funny. 'I've never been here before.' He looked so worried that Aidan stopped smiling. If Raff didn't know where they were, how would they find their way back to the Green Lake?

'I think we should look for some food or water,' Aidan said. He glanced at Warrie. Wouldn't he know how to find some? 'Will, could you and Warrie see if there's anything to eat?'

Will grinned. 'Happy I be to do that. Warrie too.' He said something to Warrie and Aidan saw a flash of a grin as the boys disappeared behind the rocks. Josie flopped down on the ground beside Jenice and the little ones. Hedley clung to Aidan's shadow. Ever since Aidan rescued him from the jack-o'-lanterns the little boy had kept close to him. Aidan looked at the kids seated there while Raff flew over the rocks trying to get his bearings.

'I don't know you all yet,' Aidan said. 'Josie, how come you are here?'

'I fell in the creek when there was a big rain. There had been a drought for years — we was all playing in the creek when the water was low. I didn't know the rain would come that day.'

'When was that?' Aidan asked.

''Twas a Saturd'y. Months ago now.'

'I mean what year, Josie.' Aidan was sure she'd know what year. She looked about ten years old, almost as old as him.

'Eighty-six, of course.' And by her full skirt and stockings, Aidan knew she meant *eighteen* hundred and eighty-six — more than a century ago.

'What about you?' Aidan pointed to a girl who hadn't spoken to him yet. She had bathers on with shorts over the top. The bathers had a frill around the neck. She looked like a picture of Aidan's mum when she was little.

'I'm Nora,' she said. 'I was swimming in the

creek. I was so excited because we were going to Adelaide the next day to see the Beatles. I like Paul best. But Trevalia is better than seeing the Beatles, I suppose … Except for the spriggans,' she added. 'Thanks for helping us.' And she smiled at Aidan shyly.

Then Hedley spoke up; he wanted Aidan to hear his story too. 'I was going to meet my pa. He was coming back from the Great War. Mother got a telegram — he was wounded and coming home. So I went to meet him. The quickest way to the main road is by crossing the creek. I didn't mean to fall in. And I still haven't found him.'

'Which great war was that, Hedley?'

Hedley looked at Aidan as if he was joking. 'There's only one Great War in the world.' Aidan stared back at Hedley with nothing to say. So he'd been here since the First World War — that was almost a century ago. He glanced across at Jenice and she raised her eyebrows at him and grinned. She'd worked all this out before.

'Don't forget Steven,' she said. 'He was looking for tadpoles, weren't you, Steven?' The little boy nodded. He was too young to know when he came and where he came from but judging by his shirt and coat and canvas sneakers, Aidan thought he was from the middle of the twentieth century. He'd seen pictures of kids dressed like that in his history book.

'I'm hungry,' is all Steven said.

Fortunately that was when Warrie and Will came back. Warrie had a dead sleepy lizard in his hand. 'Galda,' he said.

'Wait till you see this.' Will grinned as he opened his hands. The other children all said their version of 'yuck'. In Will's hands were grubs, fat white grubs.

'Barti,' Warrie said proudly. He looked as if he hadn't had one for ages and couldn't wait to sink his teeth into one.

''Ow are we going to eat 'em?' Josie asked.

'We cook 'em.' And Warrie laid the galda and some kindling down, and began rubbing two sticks together in a hollow in the ground.

There was a whoof as Raff swooped back over the group. 'Cook? Cook? We can't be staying here and setting up house. There might be danger. I have to be leading you all back to the Lady's land.'

Jenice appealed to Aidan. 'The kids are tired and they need something to eat.'

Aidan tried explaining that to Raff, but it wasn't until he said, 'What if they eat bad stuff like spriggan fruit just because they're hungry?', that Raff settled down on Aidan's shoulder and started giving hints on how to start a fire. 'Not like that. Hold the stick upright. Twist it on a piece of bark. Faster, faster.'

Warrie already knew, and he had smoke rising before the little kids got bored watching. Even Raff was impressed. 'Not a bad effort, I suppose.'

Then they watched Warrie throw the lizard in the coals. Will said something to him and Warrie threw the grubs in too. But he ate the last one raw.

'Gross,' Jenice said. 'But I guess it will help us get back to the lake. And when Warrie told them the food was ready Jenice made sure everyone had a grub each and a piece of lizard which Warrie pulled apart for them on the coals. Warrie looked as pleased as if he'd invited them all home to tea. Even Raff tried a bit. 'Not quite as good as fairy food but not bad at all,' was his verdict.

It was when they were eating the lizard that

Aidan felt something hit the back of his head. Others felt something too, for there were shouts of 'Hey, who did that?' And everyone glared around the group. There it was again — Aidan felt something small and sharp hit his neck, but this time he knew no one round the fire had done it — he'd been watching. All nine of them were present and Raff was sitting on a rock now near the fire. That meant only one thing: someone out there behind the rocks was throwing little stones at them.

Warrie made a slight noise and suddenly Aidan realised the Aboriginal boy was scared. Raff was fluttering but not flapping yet, so even he didn't know what was going on. 'What is it, Warrie?'

'Wundawinyu,' was all Warrie said. Then he said something else in his own language. Will translated, 'Warrie said they be the old spirits of the land here and they tease children.'

'Is that all they do?' Jenice asked; she drew Molly and Steven closer. Aidan wanted to know that too. And would the whistle work on them? Not likely.

Then Warrie said, 'If Wundawinyu are here, there'll be others too. And some not so happy and teasing.'

Aidan stared at the rocks behind him. He couldn't see anything there.

It was Raff who broke the silence, more thoughtfully and quietly than Aidan had ever heard him speak. 'So — the Old Ones survived after all. The Lady wondered about that.'

# Fourteen

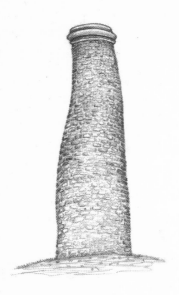

Jenice stood up. 'The children need to rest a little more. If these Wundawinyu are not dangerous, we could move to those bushes over there.' But Warrie wouldn't budge.

'Warrie won't leave the fire,' Will said.

'Why not? We have to find the lake.' Aidan stood up, ready to get on with it. They couldn't wait out here — what if night came and it wouldn't be a year-and-a-day anymore. He thought Raff would back him up, but Raff was watching Warrie, not even fiddling with his cap. Aidan had never seen him so still.

'Look!' Molly was pointing to the very bushes Jenice wanted to move towards. 'There's a scary man. Dancing in a circle.'

'Where?' Aidan couldn't see a thing, nor could Jenice but Warrie began to shiver as Hedley had done when he saw the spriggans up close. This time Raff started to flap. 'Well, what be it, boy?' And everyone looked at Warrie.

'Muripapa — they are bad and steal children.'

'Like the spriggans?' Jenice asked.

'Not bad like spriggans — not eat people. Just make 'em mad.'

'We can't go mad.' Aidan started pacing. 'We haven't time — we have to get back to the lake.' Hedley and Nora stood up too. 'I want to see the Lady,' Nora said. She sounded as if she might cry.

'Muripapa don't like fire,' Warrie said then. Nora and Hedley sat down again, a bit closer to the flames.

'What do we do now?' Jenice asked Warrie.

Warrie mumbled in his own language.

'What did he say, boy, spit it out?' Raff flew up onto Aidan's shoulder, staring at Will.

'Sometimes Epa-tura can help.'

'They sound like more bad spirits,' Aidan said.

'No. Good spirits, they will help us find the water.' Warrie glanced up then, a brighter expression on his face at last.

'How can we find them?' Aidan looked towards the bushes. He still couldn't see anything except undergrowth yet poor Molly was hiding her face in Jenice's shirt. 'How can we find something we can't see?'

'The haze in the distance,' Will explained. ''Tis them smoking their grubs to eat.'

'But if we look for a haze, we have to leave the fire,' Jenice said, glancing out at the bushes again.

'Maybe if just Warrie and I went.' And Will began to get up.

'No!' Raff stood up on Aidan's shoulder. 'No, we must be staying together but we must also be finding these Epa-tura, because I cannot help, cannot help.' He lifted off Aidan's shoulder and began flying in a circle above them, like a bird with a wounded wing.

'Raff? Are you all right?' Aidan looked up at Raff but the piskey only moaned, 'Lost, lost!'

'Okay,' Aidan said. 'Everyone stand up and hold hands. Anyone who is able to see those things in the bush, don't stare at them.' Molly kept her face burrowed into Jenice's chest so she wouldn't look by accident.

Jenice frowned at Aidan. He could tell she was going to ask how they'd get past the Muripapa just by holding hands. 'We will all sing,' Aidan said.

Will laughed. 'That is good. My da always says to sing if I am in danger,' and he started singing a song about ships and coming to South Australia: *For South Australia we are bound.* After that Aidan started 'Waltzing Matilda'.

'Never 'eard that one before,' Josie said. Will and Warrie didn't know it either, but Hedley and Nora did. Even little Steven joined in on the chorus, though Raff said it was the tune the cat died with. Aidan hoped he was joking.

Aidan wasn't sure whether the singing kept the Muripapa away or not but it took the little kids' minds off the danger. They walked for what seemed like hours, not daring to stop, even though they had to stoop under scrubby bushes and hold branches back for each other. Then the scrub started to thin out and they could walk more freely. Warrie pointed into the distance. It was Will who told them. 'See the haze on the plain — that's the Epa-tura. We be safe now.'

'I be hoping,' Raff said from Aidan's shoulder. 'I be not recognising this land.'

Aidan thought the land was a lot like the Lady's boat — it got bigger the further they went.

Warrie strode out in front of the group. The weird thing was, the closer they got to the haze the less Aidan could see it but it didn't bother Warrie. He suddenly sat on the ground and Raff told everyone to stop. Warrie bowed his head as if he was listening and then he muttered something. Finally he turned round and saw Will, then he pointed to the south. 'We go that way,' he said.

'You sure?' Aidan didn't think it looked an easy route. 'Look at all the scrub. It's worse than what we've been through. Won't the little kids' legs get scratched?'

Will said something to Warrie, but Warrie nodded and answered. 'Epa-tura say Big Water that way — only few hours away.'

''Nuff standing around doing nothing. Keep moving, keep moving,' Raff said. 'There might be more dangers.'

Aidan crouched down so Steven could climb onto his back. Then he glanced up at the sky — it was still light. He hoped Big Water meant the Green Lake. Time for him and Jenice might be running out.

# Fifteen

'I'm tired,' Molly said. Jenice had only just put her down.

'We'll have to rest again.' Jenice stroked Molly's hair that had fallen down her back.

'Rest? Rest? We can't be resting now — 'tis not a picnic. We must be finding the lake. We can't be wasting time.' Aidan wondered why Raff was so upset. Did he think time was short too?

Jenice frowned at Raff and stuck her hands

on her hips. 'We don't have wings, and the little kids' feet are aching. Some have got blisters, and I'm tired from hauling back branches in the scrub.'

'We'd be all right if we had water — not a sports bottle between us.' Aidan always took water with him everywhere at home. Home. How far away was home? Were they still within the mine area?

Raff regarded Jenice for a full minute. 'All right. You all rest. 'Tis checking the lay of the land I be. Back dreckly,' and he flew up over the bushes out of sight, but he returned before the little kids even got settled on the ground. Aidan heard the beating of his wings. When he was happy or excited they sounded like a miniature helicopter. 'The Old Ones were right!' Raff was laughing, flying around all their heads, brushing their hair with his wings. It made the children giggle. 'I know where we are — we are close to the Lady's land. We be right as ninepence now.'

Raff made everyone forget their tired legs and thirstiness — they all got up and started walking, even Molly, with Raff flying ahead. It wasn't long before Jenice and Aidan could see a metallic green through the scrub as it thinned. 'It's the lake,' Jenice cried and everyone cheered, even Raff.

He settled on Aidan's shoulder and sniffed like a dog. 'Oh, the Lady's land smells as sweet as new hay. Happy as a duck I be.'

Aidan never knew he'd be so glad to see those lilac cliffs again; the copper green of the water seemed so familiar now. The younger children were as excited as Aidan was when he came home after a holiday to see Bridie. Except the nine of them hadn't been on a holiday. Aidan never wanted to see another spriggan or have another adventure in his whole life.

'Let's let the kids rest a bit,' Jenice said, flopping on the grass near the lake. 'The boat's still here at least.' It didn't take long for Warrie and Will to find a spring nearby so everyone could have a drink, and for Raff to think up a joke.

'What be a spriggan's favourite game?'

'Swallow the leader,' Will said. Aidan wondered if he'd heard Raff tell it before.

'What be the name of a piskey who rolls around in the leaves?'

Aidan groaned. 'I've heard that one in my school even. Russell.'

But nothing seemed to bother Raff. He laughed so hard at the joke himself, he rolled on the ground too. Then he got the hiccups. That made the little kids laugh.

Aidan sat watching the kids giggling. 'We'll have to row across at least twice to get all the kids across to the Lady's cave.'

'No problem,' Raff said, between hiccups. 'We'll all — hic — fit.'

Aidan remembered when he first came to the lake and he put his foot in the boat — it seemed bigger. Could it happen again? With nine of them? Aidan looked up at the sky. When did the sun set here? Surely he'd been here longer than a day but he hadn't had a sleep yet. Suddenly he yawned. Perhaps he shouldn't think about it. Raff stirred on the ground, patting the grass with his hands.

'We be — hic — safe now,' and he sighed as though he had walked all the way from the Dark Bush and not sat on Aidan's shoulder through most of it. Safety was on Aidan's mind too as he watched the lake. It was as smooth as his bathroom mirror at the moment but what if those ripples started up again? He caught Jenice staring at him. She was tired but she had that same look in her eyes when she would come to his cubby and say, 'Let's do something exciting today.' He took a big breath; he hadn't braved the spriggans' under-world to let some ripples spook him.

They may as well get it over with. He stood up and Raff fluttered up to his shoulder. 'Come on then.' All the kids followed him to the water's edge.

Nora looked wistfully at the water lapping at her toes. 'I wish I could swim in it.'

'No.' Aidan was sharp. 'No one's swimming in it. We have to get across to the cave quickly.'

Raff was right about the boat — as soon as one of the children put their foot in the boat there seemed to be enough room for all of them. Soon all nine of them were perched on the benches. Aidan took the oars and Jenice promised to take a turn; so did Will. Raff sat in the stern, his hiccups gone, and as he rowed Aidan could see the piskey's grinning face.

It was when they were halfway across that

Aidan noticed the ripple. At first he thought he must have imagined it, but then he saw it again. He glanced up and saw Raff looking at him strangely, then the piskey said quite conversationally, 'There be a giant in the lake.'

'What?' Aidan almost lost his hold on the oars. He glanced at the other kids. They all heard but no one else seemed very worried yet. 'What do you mean?'

Raff was enjoying himself. 'His name be Trebiggan. People in Cornwall thought he were dead, but he followed a ship to this place and on the way he were in the sea so long he grew a merman's tail. Iss, a long tail like a giant shark.'

Aidan was watching the ripples. 'Jenice? Do you know about it?'

'I've never seen it. We've always been with the Lady. She brought us across the day we went picking fruit.'

'But we went too far that day,' Josie added. They all shuddered. Aidan was surprised that the thought of the spriggans could bring a shudder and not the ripples on the lake. At least on land you had a chance. If the giant came out of the water while they were still on the lake, what would they do?

'Why didn't you tell me?' Aidan asked Raff, his voice rising a tone.

'You didn't ask.'

'I asked if it was safe.'

'Well it is — usually.'

Aidan half closed his eyes. 'What does "usually" mean?'

'Usually, he's in a good mood. Of course they tell horrible stories about giants.'

Aidan nodded; he'd read a few himself.

'About giants eating children. They said Trebiggan used to roast them on a rock outside his cave in Cornwall.'

'You should have warned me before I brought the kids onto the lake.'

'Oh, that was before he came here. We don't believe those stories any more.'

Aidan felt light-headed all of a sudden. Here he was, rowing in a tiny boat on a copper lake with kids who should be dead and a piskey saying some stories weren't true. Aidan shook himself, wiped his eyes with his upper arm. Was he, Aidan, real?

He felt the splashes on his hands as he pulled at the oars. Yes, he was still there, in a little rowboat with eight other kids and a piskey in the middle of a copper lake with ripples and bubbles coming closer and closer. Aidan pulled harder on the oars, but he was tiring. Jenice moved beside him to take one.

'Faster, Jenice. We have to beat the ripples.'

'There be no need to rush,' Raff said. He was laughing. How strange. Why wasn't he flapping as he usually did when there was danger?

'The ripples are coming closer!'

'No need —'

And suddenly he was there — the giant. He surged up out of the water, so close he made the boat rock as if it was a toy in a bathtub. 'Row, row!' Aidan shouted. 'We're going to capsize. Everyone lean to the right.' All the kids leant over to keep the boat upright. The giant shook his head and a shower of water rained on them. It was like being on the open sea in a storm. Josie screamed and all the little kids started howling. Jenice's mouth dropped open as she stared up at the giant as high as the mine chimney.

'You should have warned us,' Aidan shouted. 'Isn't there another way to the cave?'

'No.'

Aidan couldn't understand why Raff wasn't yet in a full flap. The waves died down and the giant sank under the water until just his chest and head and long arms were showing. He glided closer to the boat; it made the little kids scream louder.

Raff called to the children. 'No need to screech like cats in a bonfire.'

'Then do something,' Aidan said.

'No need …'

'Ho,' Trebiggan thundered. 'Human children on my lake.'

Aidan didn't care for the giant's tone. 'We're friends of the Lady. Isn't it the Lady's lake?' he shouted, so the giant could hear.

The giant brought his head closer. 'Friends? Hmm. What's the Lady's is mine too, see.'

Aidan turned to Raff. 'He protects the lake?'

Raff nodded. 'You could be saying that.'

'The cave too?'

He glanced slyly at Aidan. 'Iss, 'tis why there be no need to fear.'

The giant's hand came down closer, scooped up the boat. Now Aidan felt as dizzy as he did on the Big Dipper at the show and all the kids squealed. Trebiggan set the boat on the shore, near the cave. He chuckled; to Aidan it sounded like a rumble of thunder. He felt like making some thunder himself. How dare Raff play with them like that. The giant said, 'You didn't have to row the whole way, children.'

'See, he be our friend,' Raff said.

As soon as the boat was steady on the ground, Aidan dived for Raff and caught him around the middle. He felt like grabbing him by the neck and squeezing hard. Instead he shook him until his silly little beanie fell off. 'Why didn't you say? You did that on purpose, didn't you? You little p-pesky piskey. Scared us for nothing.'

It was Will who answered. 'He's only a piskey, Aidan. They like to have a joke.' He picked up Raff's cap and placed it back on his head.

Aidan let Raff go and the piskey hovered above them. His wings fluttered more slowly than usual, but Aidan tried not to notice. They all watched Trebiggan swim away. His fish tail broke the surface like a killer whale's; he made the huge lake look as small as a backyard pool.

'Why didn't he come out before?' Aidan asked, more quietly this time.

Raff floated down onto Aidan's shoulder. But he didn't sit and settle as he usually did — he balanced on one leg, ready to fly off again. 'He be checking. When the Lady be in the boat he doesn't need to surface.' Raff kept glancing at the side of Aidan's face and grinning like a sheep, but Aidan didn't smile back.

'The lake must be really deep to hide him,' Jenice said with awe in her tone.

'Oh, the lake be bottomless. It opens onto another land and goes out to the sea. Trebiggan has a cave down there somewhere. I heard tell he sleeps a lot.' Then Raff added in Aidan's ear, 'You be in a proper boil, boy. I never meant any harm.'

Aidan tried to smile then. At least Raff was trying to be friendly again. He helped Will and Warrie drag the boat up to the mooring post. Raff directed from Aidan's neck and told them to knot the rope to keep it secure. Then they all made their way up to the cave. Molly and Nora skipped on ahead and Aidan grinned at them. 'Now we're back we'll find out if Josie's right about the year-and-a-day and if Jenice can go home. A sleep first would be good.'

'Not if you be wanting to take Jenice home.' Raff flew off Aidan's shoulder and buzzed in his face.

Aidan stopped short. What was Raff up to now? 'What do you mean?'

'You said it be a year-and-a-day since Jenice left your land?'

'Yes.'

'The Lady will be knowing this so don't be going to sleep when the children do.'

'Why should it matter?'

'If you sleep it won't be a year-and-a-day any more — 'twill be a year and two days.'

Aidan stared at him, horrified. 'So that's how time works in Trevalia?'

Raff nodded his head so hard his cap nearly fell off again.

'Then Jenice couldn't leave with me.' Aidan glanced at her; she had a frown between her eyes. Did Raff know what he was saying? Was he joking? Or did he feel so bad about frightening them on the lake that he was helping them to go home? Then Aidan saw Will's disbelieving face.

'Why are you warning me, Raff? The Lady won't be happy with you.'

Raff laughed. 'I be knowing you now, boy, and I know you will not be telling. Listen, the Lady will be understanding you want to go home; she'll try to keep you but she has no power over you for you walked across the stones. But beware, you must never let her be knowing you want to take Jenice.'

Then Raff flew in a circle above Aidan's head and hovered in front of his face again. 'And don't be worrying, boy. I will be helping.'

# Sixteen

There wasn't time to make plans, for the Lady appeared before they reached the mouth of the cave, welcoming them and kissing the little ones. 'I knew you would not fail, Aidan Curnow. Come. We have a gathering in your honour.' They followed her into the main quartz cave. She clapped her hands and music began. 'We shall have a great party,' she said. Her eyes were sparkling but for the first time Aidan thought they were hard as well as shiny. 'First, you must all wash. There are bowls of spring water in your room.'

In the cave, Aidan and Jenice made plans, while Josie helped the younger children wash. 'She's not going to let us go,' Jenice said first. 'Not me, anyway, I can tell.'

Will was close enough to overhear. 'The rest of us want to stay here. We like the Lady and if what you say be true about the mine closing and things being different, 'tis best we stay.' He had a strange look on his face, not quite as if he was going to cry but almost. It made Aidan wonder if he'd realised his parents and all the people he knew were dead after all.

Then Will said, 'She does love us — you too.'

'Is that love — stopping you from going home when you want to? Shouldn't she be happy for Jenice and me?'

'She gets lonely without 'uman children,' Josie said; then her voice choked a bit. 'She's like our own mam.' Aidan tried not to stare at Josie. It sounded as if she also knew she didn't have a mother of her own anymore.

'I think it's a good idea that you stay,' he said.

'Besides, if what you said earlier is true about the year-and-a-day, only Jenice can go anyway.'

Then Will moved closer. 'You mustn't drink the hot fruit drink.'

'At the party?' Aidan asked.

'No, afterwards. The Lady sometimes gives us a drink before sleeping — it makes us rest. If she thinks you are planning to go, she'll surely give you one tonight.'

'I remember now.' Jenice picked up a towel and dried her face. 'When I first came the Lady gave me that to drink and I forgot about Mum and trying to get home.'

'You will surely sleep if you drink it,' Will said.

'And Raff said I mustn't go to sleep.'

'Can we trust him?' Jenice handed the towel to Aidan.

'Can't think what else to do right now. He said he'd help.'

'You'll be okay though — you walked across the creek. The Lady wanted you to come to save us from the spriggans. She can't keep you even if you do fall asleep.'

'But you won't be able to come with me,

Jenice. We'll have to be careful. She knows everything —'

'Even what we think.'

'So we think of something else —' said Aidan,
'— pretend we don't know you are able to go. Act
confident. We mustn't show any fear.' Already he
felt the familiar shivers like a hundred legs uncurling and digging into his middle.

The Lady had prepared a huge feast, even
bigger than when Aidan first came. It was certain
she was pleased all the children were back in the
cave. She was smiling at Aidan as though he was
already her new son, and it was all Aidan could do
to stop himself from putting a few things straight,
like telling her he had parents of his own and he
meant to get back to them as soon as possible.

The music and dancing were as before, but
there was more food. There were tables stacked
with it; it reminded Aidan of a wedding he'd been
to once. First of all, the Lady asked Aidan for her
tin whistle back. She had a firm look on her face
and he handed it over reluctantly. He'd been
hoping she would forget about it. He'd need it if
he and Jenice were to escape and find their way

through the knockers' tunnels. Then the Lady made sure all the children had a mountain of food in front of them. The piskeys flew down to bring more fruit or fairy bread if the children managed to look even slightly hungry. Aidan felt himself getting fuller and wondered if it was dangerous to eat it. Raff hadn't said anything about the food. Aidan saw the Lady watching him and he tried not to think about it. He smiled at a small person in a pink sparkly ball gown sitting on the other side of the table. 'What's your name?'

'Flora. I'm really a Browney. When I were younger I'd come to your land and clean up messy houses and feed forgotten babies.'

'Really?' Aidan said politely. Wouldn't it be nice if someone like her cleaned up his room? 'How long have you been here?'

'Ever since the Lady came — we all travelled with her on the ship long ago.' The small woman sounded like Raff when Aidan asked him that a few days ago — how long ago was that in his own time? How much time would have passed when he finally got home? Would he be the opposite of that Rip Van Winkle story, being younger while all his friends were so much older? He looked up; Jenice was frowning at him. The Lady was watching him too. And this time she wasn't smiling. He mustn't think of 'how long' or about home, just about the food and being happy here. What if she knew he was going to take Jenice with him and she put a guard or a spell on the cave door? Or gave him that drink? How could he not drink it? Let it dribble down the inside of his shirt? What if she stayed to make sure he had drunk it? The Lady was capable of anything.

'Raff, tell us a joke,' he said. Raff's jokes were pretty corny but maybe it would stop him thinking about leaving with Jenice.

'What be the name of a small person with no arms or legs in the lake?'

'Bob!' yelled a piskey.

'Why does the dragaroo have a long neck?'

'Because its feet stink,' shouted a small man.

'What be the same size and shape as Trebiggan but weighs nothing?'

Jenice knew that one. 'His shadow.'

Everyone laughed, even the Lady. It sounded like water tinkling into a pond. But Aidan couldn't find anything funny. What if he fell asleep before anything happened? Raff was staring at him now from the air and making faces at him when the Lady wasn't looking, but Aidan just yawned. He caught Jenice frowning at him and he stifled the next one — he couldn't fail now after all that had happened. Then he thought of his mum. What was she doing, was she sad like Mrs Trengove? Was she missing him? And without his intending it, an image of Jenice's mother sadly shopping slipped into his mind.

# Seventeen

The Lady clapped her hands and the music stopped. 'It is time now for you to sleep. Human children need more sleep than piskeys and small people.' Aidan was sure she was looking at him as she said that. 'We thank you again, Aidan Curnow, for your service to Trevalia. I can see that you want to go home?' She said it as a question and Aidan nodded. What was the point of denying it? The Lady's eyes lost a little of their shine. 'Then you will travel more safely after sleeping. Goodnight, children.' Everyone said 'goodnight' and the sound was like a thousand butterflies and tiny birds flittering in the air.

As they walked out of the sparkling cave the music started again and the piskeys began dancing in the air. Aidan could hear the Lady calling to Raff to get her some more fairy bread. Aidan's legs wobbled in a crooked line to the children's cave. 'Come on,' Jenice said and she took his hand. Aidan was too tired to mind.

'I think she knows,' he said.

'It wouldn't surprise me. You looked so sad, what were you thinking of?'

'Our mothers.'

'Mine too?' Jenice turned to face him. 'Oh, Aidan, she'll catch on for sure that I want to go.'

'I'm sorry. I was so tired — I couldn't help it.'

'Look, here we are — I'll get the little ones into bed. You'd better help so you don't nod off.'

Aidan helped Steven pull off his shorts and shirt and put on a shift that the small people had made. It glistened and looked as if it was made from the ore in the rock walls, yet it also felt like the soft things his mother wore to bed. When Steven lay down he said sleepily, 'See you in the morning, Aidan.'

Aidan hesitated. Hedley was watching him. He couldn't tell the younger kids he was going, nor could Jenice surely? What if the Lady came in to say goodnight and she read their minds? 'Sure, Steven. It was great meeting you.'

Jenice was putting Molly to bed when Aidan looked up and noticed she was crying. 'Jenice?' He went over to her.

'I feel as if I've known these kids forever. They're like my brothers and sisters. Dear little Molly.' For one awful moment Aidan thought Jenice would change her mind and stay, but she blew her nose and whispered, 'I'll miss them so much.'

'Why are you crying?' Nora asked from her petal-filled mattress.

'Because I love you.'

Nora smiled. 'I love you too, Jenice. You're nicer than the big sister I had before.'

Jenice turned to Josie. 'I'll miss you,' she said, more quietly. 'Josie?'

'Yes, Jenice?'

'Don't tell them till tomorrow. It might be dangerous if they know. Tell them that it was hard for me to go, that I'll always remember them, but my mum must be so sad. I have to see her. I'm all she's got.'

Josie put her arms around Jenice. 'I understand,' she said. And Aidan knew she did understand about Trevalia after all — that she would always be a child while the rest of the world spun out its days and years and grew old.

Just then Hedley ran up to Aidan and threw his arms around his middle. 'You are leaving, aren't you?' he whispered.

Aidan still didn't want to say so in case the Lady asked Hedley later. He had to live here afterwards. 'I will miss you, Hedley. I wish you were my little brother,' was all he said.

'I am already.' Hedley was grinning now. 'I'll always be here. You can come and visit.' Aidan looked at him in surprise. It was something he had never thought of. Will slipped over to him then.

'What is it like now — the town?' he asked quietly. Aidan wasn't sure what to say. How could he tell Will that he went to school with his great-something nephew? Or tell Warrie that he was the last of his people to be alive?

'Is your last name Jones?' Will nodded. So Will *was* Chris Jones's great-great uncle who was lost years ago as Josh said, but Aidan didn't know how to explain that. 'Um, the roads are bigger, I think. There's a big school.' Should he tell him about cars?

'Are there steam trains yet? I heard talk of them.'

'There used to be — they've gone now,' Aidan said carefully. Will looked disappointed and Aidan thought it might be best to leave it at that. If he told Will about cars and planes and huge ships with no sails, he might want to go and see. And how could he leave? If any of the kids left would they die because they were in the wrong time? Aidan glanced at Jenice. What about her — would the year-and-a-day magic that Josie heard about keep her safe?

Jenice came closer and smiled. 'Why so worried?'

Just then Warrie called softly from the doorway, 'The Lady is comin'.'

Josie, Will and Warrie, still in his possum skin, dived into their beds and only Jenice and Aidan were sitting on theirs, fully clothed, when the Lady walked in with a copper jug and two large tumblers on a quartz tray. For that split instant Aidan wished Raff was there. Jenice and Will would say he was just a piskey, but he said he would help. Where was he?

The Lady was smiling at them, but Aidan didn't trust the smile. He was looking at the jug. 'Now,' the Lady said. 'You have both been through a lot and are overtired so I've brought you a little nightcap. We are so thankful to you, Aidan Curnow. You don't need to go when you wake up. Stay awhile with us — I have a surprise planned. For I have something special I would like to present to you. There is no reason to go so soon, is there?'

It sounded so interesting and sensible — so soothing. Of course it would be better to go after a good sleep. It was the sort of thing his own mother would say. What would it matter surely? Could you believe piskeys? Look how Raff teased them about the giant. He might be doing the same about the Lady. And Josie might have it wrong about the year-and-a-day — it was just a story really. The Lady poured gold liquid into the tumblers and held one out to Aidan. He couldn't refuse or the Lady would know he'd been warned. She was still smiling as though she knew he would drink it. The tumbler was like an eggcup in his hand. Maybe it wouldn't have much effect on him. There was no way he could throw it away — the Lady was too close. She'd see if he poured it down his shirt or threw it over his back. It worked in all the movies he'd seen but in real life it didn't at all. There was no way out. He felt a flutter of fear. What if it made him stay there forever like the other kids? He heard Will turn in his bed and make a slight noise. Will had said not to drink it.

Then the Lady was looking into Aidan's eyes and smiling. 'And what would be so terrible about staying with me, Aidan? Together we would have power over everything in Trevalia, even the spriggans. Did you know they guard treasure?' Did she say that or did he think it? Aidan wasn't sure. He only knew that suddenly he could hear music in his head and he felt fine. He drank the liquid in one gulp — it burned a bit and felt hot once it hit his stomach but it chased all the shivers and flutters away.

'Jenice?' The Lady smiled at her as she too drank the liquid. 'I love you too much to let you go, Jenice. The other world is a difficult place, an evil place. You will be happier and safer here.' Jenice's eyes were almost closed as the Lady stood up to go. 'You will both thank me later.'

Aidan watched her glide out of the cave. Once she'd gone he suddenly felt the quiver in his stomach again. What had he done? He wasn't supposed to drink it. The Lady knew everything he thought and took his willpower away. He'd failed Jenice and maybe himself too. He tried to keep his eyes from closing but they felt like the bonnet of a car with its spring gone. How could he keep awake? 'Jenice?' But she didn't answer. Will was whispering to him but he couldn't understand.

Just as Aidan felt the darkness wrap closer around him, he heard the whirring of wings. 'Raff?' But he couldn't even raise his head.

'Boy, oh, boy, all be not lost, not lost. Here, I

have the remedy to break the power of the draught.'

Aidan managed to prise open one eye and there was Raff hovering in front of his face, his arms full. 'Here, you must be chewing this. I hope I am not too late. Not too late.' Raff put the thing, the size of a small thin wafer, into Aidan's mouth. 'Eat it boy, quickly, quickly. 'Twill reverse the drink's power and keep you awake. For a time.'

Aidan chewed while Raff opened Jenice's mouth. She must have been slightly awake for her mouth worked and slowly she woke properly. Aidan too. He sat up. 'I tried not to drink it, but it's like I forgot how dangerous it was with the Lady there.' Then he looked crossly at Raff. 'Where were you? You said you'd help.'

Raff managed to look slightly hurt. 'And so I be here helping.'

'How long will the biscuit last?'

'I not be knowing that — we haven't used it before.'

Aidan spluttered. 'I'm a guinea pig?'

'I not be knowing about guinea pigs either, but we'll be sitting ducks if we don't leave now.'

Aidan and Jenice both stood up — they took a wobbly step, while Raff swooped around them. 'What will the Lady say when she finds out!' For Aidan was sure now the Lady could find out anything.

'The Lady be only doing what she thinks will be helping. She has never hurt anyone.'

'So why are you doing this? Doesn't the Lady know best?' Aidan knew he was being mean, but Raff didn't seem to be annoyed.

'I've spent more time with you than the Lady has, boy.' And with that he chuckled. Then he was suddenly serious. 'You be on your own now. If you had waited and gone later, the Lady would have given you a gift to ensure your safety from Trevalia, but since you cannot wait, 'twill be harder for you. There may be more trials.' Raff didn't say what they were but Aidan thought first of the dragaroo, and what about those tunnels where the knockers were?

'What if you came too?' Aidan asked.

At that Raff looked away and began flying up and down above their heads. 'That is one thing I cannot do. Cannot do.' He groaned. 'The Lady will be knowing I am gone. She may call for extra help — it could be worse for you.' Aidan didn't ask again. Raff had risked a lot already by helping them. 'The party be still raging,' Raff said. He floated down to Aidan's shoulder and put a skinny arm around Aidan's neck. 'They will not hear you. I will show you a secret passage, but more than that I must not do. Must not do.'

Raff looked so worried. It was an expression Aidan wished he could wipe away. 'We'll be okay,' he said to make Raff feel better.

'I be hoping so,' Raff said without his usual laugh. 'It won't be all beer and skittles, boy, that be certain.'

# Eighteen

'This way, boy, this way.' Raff kept his voice low. Aidan and Jenice followed him as he flew in front. Aidan didn't feel tired anymore, but he wondered how long it took for the wafer Raff gave him to wear off. Raff showed them another passageway Aidan hadn't noticed before, that skirted around the main cave. They could hear the music and singing even though the walls were made of rock.

As they climbed up some steps, Aidan said, 'This is the way we came in.'

'Shh.' Raff glanced back at them. 'The entrance to the main cave be right beside you.'

That kept Aidan and Jenice quiet, though Aidan didn't think anyone from the cave would hear much above all that music.

Outside they could see the lake, shining green. 'Doesn't the sun set here at all?' Aidan asked.

'I've never been out after the Lady puts us to bed,' Jenice said. 'I've never seen it dark.'

'The days be long here.' Raff nodded his head, yet his cap stayed on. 'Trevalia be a land of light and happiness.'

Aidan didn't argue but he wondered why — if it was so good — he was so intent on helping them leave. Raff settled onto Aidan's shoulder and put both little arms around his neck and squeezed. 'I be hoping you come back, boy.'

'Thanks.' Aidan smiled politely but he doubted he'd ever return.

'The boat's still there,' Jenice said. And with that, Raff said 'goodbye' and flew around their heads a few times and then back into the lilac mountain. As Aidan watched him go the quivering started up in his stomach again. Would they find the way to the creek? Raff and the music had always guided him before.

'Come on.' Jenice held the boat steady as Aidan climbed in, then she jumped in and they took an oar each. 'I'll help — the sooner we get away the better. The Lady might have some plan if she finds we are gone.'

'Does she go into the children's cave in the night?'

'Sometimes. Once I was awake and she came in to tuck everyone in. Maybe she does it a lot.'

'Then let's row harder.'

It wasn't until they were over halfway across and Aidan was beginning to relax that he saw the first ripple. The giant. How could he have forgotten about him? He may have been friendly but what if the Lady had warned him to keep watch in case they escaped? The ripple turned into a whirlpool and all of sudden he was there. His head and arms were above water, making the boat rock. No time to row faster and reach the shore.

Trebiggan reached out one long arm and put a finger on the boat's stern. It bobbed up and down, and water splashed on Aidan from the wash that the giant had caused.

'What now?' Jenice mouthed.

'Ho, children on my lake.'

Aidan wished the giant didn't sound so loud. He glanced back to the Lady's cave. No one showed in the dark hollow in the cliff.

'We're the Lady's friends,' Jenice said, loudly enough for him to hear. 'You saw us last time.'

'Lady's friends is it? Then why do you have no guide? Hmm?'

'Guide?' Aidan frowned at Jenice.

'He means Raff.'

'The Lady never sends anyone on the lake without a guide. Methinks you are running away. Hmm?' If it weren't so serious, Aidan would have smiled. Trebiggan looked like his dad when Aidan was trying to get out of the dishes, and he escaped through the toilet window to find his dad was out there waiting. But a giant wasn't like a dad.

'What are you going to do?' Aidan asked. 'Please let us pass to the other side.'

''Tis not safe by the creek, if that is where you are headed,' Trebiggan answered. 'I will keep you safe until a guide comes.'

Jenice stifled a cry. 'How will he keep us safe? We can't go under water.'

'I think the Lady's warned him and he's going to hold us until she comes. How did she do that, I wonder?'

'She knows everything — we were crazy to think this would work.'

'Come, my beauties. Just hold your breath a little while.' Aidan watched, terrified, as the giant's hands came down and picked each of them up and tucked them under his arms.

This time Jenice screamed. 'I don't like the water.'

'Hold your nose,' was all Aidan had time to say as the giant plunged down into the lake. They felt the water push against them when the giant's tail slapped the surface as he submerged. Jenice squeezed her eyes shut but Aidan's were open. Not that he could see much. The water was thick and green, and they went so fast his ears felt tight and full. Then they seemed to travel sideways and they surfaced into an underwater cave. Both Jenice and Aidan gulped in great breaths of air.

'You stay here and rest,' Trebiggan said, shaking his long hair dry and wetting them all the more, 'and I'll look for something you'll like to eat. Don't think I have any dry clothes though. You look like ducks in a thunderstorm.'

'Everyone wants us to go to sleep,' Aidan grumbled when Trebiggan had slithered away. 'And everyone in this land lives in caves, talks about ducks, and only thinks about food.'

Jenice was looking at the dark water all around. 'How can we escape from here?'

'He's not likely to take us back, that's for sure.' Aidan slumped down on the floor.

'You don't suppose he will eat us, do you?'

'N–no, I don't think so. Wouldn't the Lady be cross with him if he ate us?'

'Yes, but what if he never told her. Aidan, she'd just decide we made it home.'

Aidan didn't want to think about what the giant might or mightn't do — they had to think of a way to get back to the boat. 'Look, I think we should have a rest and think about what we can do.' In a little while Jenice closed her eyes. Aidan didn't dare do that, for Jenice wouldn't be able to leave Trevalia if he fell asleep. He wished everything didn't depend on him and he was back with his mum and dad, and his dad could take care of the giant. But his dad wasn't there. 'Hey.' It was the thought of his dad that gave him the idea. That time they had those holidays at Moonta Bay. His dad had taken him snorkelling one afternoon, and they'd found a little cave among the rocks where the fish swam in and out.

'Jenice. I know what we have to do.'

She yawned. 'What?'

'We have to get to the surface. I've done it with Dad, snorkelling.'

'But we don't have air or goggles or anything.'

'I don't think it's that far. Remember? When Trebiggan brought us down, did you run out of air?'

'No, but he was going fast, and he's bigger than us. It'd take us longer to go the same distance.'

'But we have to try. Don't you want to see your mum?'

Jenice nodded miserably.

'Then we have to take a risk. I don't know how long Raff's remedy will last, and then our chance will be gone. Trebiggan's just going to keep us here until I fall asleep, I'm sure of it. Jenice, you can do anything, remember. You even taught me how to ride a bike. You got me to climb the plane tree in the Institute garden. You told me not to be a scaredy cat. Remember the day we were on Ross Creek bridge and I fell off? You got me home, remember? We can do this.'

'I can't,' Jenice whispered. 'We might drown. I almost drowned in the creek — it was the most dreadful feeling. I couldn't breathe. I couldn't stand it — it hurt, the water rushing in, choking. Until I heard the music. And all of a sudden I could get out of the water, my foot found a rock to step on. I followed the music and there was the Lady by the lake, playing her whistle. She saved my life — I should have told her I was going.'

'Jenice, think. We can do this, we'll hold hands —'

'What? And sing?'

Aidan hesitated. Was she joking or still upset?

'You can do it, Jenice. If we stay here you won't get home.'

She sighed. Aidan waited. 'Okay, but don't you let my hand go.'

'Don't forget, we've had fairy food. Raff told me last time I ate it that it makes us stronger. Come on.' They walked over to the huge pool, big enough for a giant. Aidan thought the cave was like the airlock in a submarine. Once they jumped into the pool they'd be in a wide passageway and they would have to swim out to the lake and then head upwards to the surface.

'What if we come across the giant?'

'He's gone the other way, into the caves,' Aidan said. 'I heard him slithering for ages with that fishtail of his. I'll count to three, right?'

'Okay.'

But when Aidan took Jenice's hand it was shaking. He squeezed it and grinned, trying to ignore his own quivery insides. 'We'll be okay. One. Two. Three!' And they jumped. Jenice had hold of her nose with the other hand, but soon found she had to help push the water back as Aidan swam along the huge water-filled passageway. Then the water seemed a lighter colour and they emerged into the lake. Aidan pushed his free arm up to the surface, kicking his feet. Jenice did the same. But she was right — it took them a lot longer to go up than it had taken to plunge down with the giant.

Aidan's lungs felt as if they were about to burst like a thinly stretched balloon by the time he could see they were nearly there. He broke the surface and pulled Jenice up beside him. She was spluttering and hanging onto him so hard she was pushing him under. 'Jenice. Stop it, we're safe now. The boat's not far off.' But Jenice didn't stop pulling at him even when he tried to guide her towards the boat. He couldn't think of anything else to do except smack her face hard. It was as if she just woke up from a nightmare. 'You hit me.'

'I'm sorry, I had to. You were dragging us both under. Look, the boat's over there. Hang on to me and I'll swim over.' This time Jenice didn't struggle but managed to kick so they went faster. Aidan didn't want the giant suddenly finding them gone and surfacing with a bellow before they could get off the lake.

The oars were still in their rowlocks. Aidan pushed Jenice up into the boat and then she helped pull him in. 'This reminds me of when you came and pulled me up onto my cubby that day.'

Jenice grinned. 'It seems so long ago.'

'Just over a year.'

'Quick, let's row,' Jenice said then. They had nearly reached the shore and Aidan was sure they'd made it when Jenice pointed behind them. 'What's that?'

Aidan looked round and groaned. The ripples were in the middle of the lake but they were following them. It wouldn't take the giant long to catch up to them. 'Row faster, Jenice. It's Trebiggan. We're nearly there.' They pulled and pulled. Aidan tried not to look backwards. All he thought about was getting to the shore, and when they reached it with a bump, he almost forgot where he was.

'Aidan. Aidan. Help me drag the boat up.' Just then Trebiggan's head surfaced not ten metres from them in the deeper water.

'Why are you going? I only wanted to help. Come back, and I'll help you.'

'It's all right,' Aidan said to Jenice, 'he can't come out — he's got a fishtail.'

'He's got long arms though', and Jenice walked steadily backwards.

Aidan didn't know whether to believe Trebiggan or not. What if his help was just like the Lady's? She said she loved them but she wouldn't let them go. Raff told jokes and teased them. But he did help in the end, didn't he? But Aidan didn't think the giant would — he didn't know them like Raff did. Aidan turned away from the lake.

Now they had to make for the creek, but first they had to find the tunnels where the knockers were and then navigate their way through them. How on earth would they do that without music to guide them?

# Nineteen

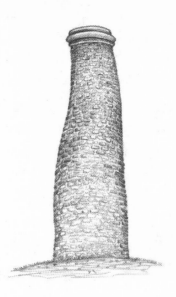

The entrance was close to the lake, Aidan remembered that much. They found another spring like the one Warrie found on the other side. Jenice had a drink while Aidan looked for the shaft — for wasn't that all it was? A hole in the ground with hundreds of steps leading below? 'I've found it!' Jenice was right behind him.

She looked down at the bits of wood wedged into the rock below. 'Is it safe?'

'I came this way. Didn't you?'

'I don't remember. I only heard the music like in a dream and I woke up when I reached the lake and saw the Lady.'

'Come on. We can't hang around. The Lady might have more tricks up her sleeve.' And Aidan lowered himself into the hole, putting his first foot on a step, and down he went. Jenice came in above him, hanging onto the ropes on the sides. 'There are a lot of steps.'

'It was worse going up.'

Soon they reached the bottom and a passage-way spread out in front of them. Aidan had thought about it while he was coming down. 'I reckon we'll just follow the main passageway.' The glistening on the walls was still there as Aidan remembered it and it offered a little light to show their way.

'At least it's not as dark as the spriggans' caves,' Jenice observed. Aidan didn't want to be reminded of the spriggans right then. He kept listening for any sounds, but the walls were silent. They walked steadily until they reached the end of the passage, then the trouble started. There were two tunnels the same width. Jenice voiced Aidan's fear. 'How do we know which is the main one?'

Aidan didn't know. 'We'll have to guess and hope it's the right way. We have a fifty-fifty chance.' It was at the end of the next passage that they heard the knocking.

'What's that noise?' Jenice asked.

Aidan had put off telling her but he had to now. 'It's the knockers. They live down here. They still work the mine.'

Jenice stood in front of him so he had to stop. 'You mean they're like the spriggans?'

'N–no, I don't think so. When I was here with Raff we left them food and they liked it. I saw one — it wasn't scary like the spriggans. I hope they'll let us pass.' Aidan didn't say he thought the knocker was scary when he first saw it — just in comparison with the spriggans a knocker didn't seem so scary anymore.

'What if we get the tunnels wrong and we don't "pass through" and we end up in their home or something? What will they do then?'

Aidan had to be honest. 'I don't know. We just have to try.' He thought this was the scariest thing yet — they were all alone in a strange land with nothing or no one to help them. They kept feeling their way forward and tried not to notice the noise that sounded as if it was on the other side of the rock wall, as if whatever was making it could come crashing through at any moment. He didn't dare say what he was truly scared of — that they could get trapped underground forever, wandering blindly, never finding the end. It could be like a maze. With no opening at the end. Suddenly, Aidan sank down onto the ground.

Jenice was a few steps in front before she realised he wasn't with her. 'Aidan? Aidan. You can't give up now. We've been through everything — the spriggans, the giant. You're so brave. We can do this too.'

Aidan looked up at Jenice. 'You're wrong, you know.'

'What about?' Jenice was ready for an argument; she had her hands on her hips.

But Aidan was determined not to be scared of her too. 'I'm not brave at all. I know the Lady thinks I am though she should know better — she can see into people's minds. Every time we've had to do something new I've been so scared I wanted to go to the toilet — this dreadful, quivery feeling in my stomach all the time.'

'Yet you go ahead and do it. Once the action starts you get into whatever you have to do.'

'But I don't feel brave.'

'Did you think I was brave when we jumped into the water in Trebiggan's cave?'

'Of course, that was so brave after you nearly drowned in the creek.'

'See? I didn't feel brave at all. Maybe all brave people don't realise they are.'

Aidan grinned. 'You always did make me feel better.' Then he stood up. 'But I wish Raff was here. He could tell us which tunnel to take. We could be here for ages. Raff, where are you?'

'At least we've got each other.'

That made Aidan laugh properly. 'If you're not feeling brave I can help you and vice versa, eh?'

'So long as you don't go to sleep we'll be okay.'

Aidan didn't need to remind her that they didn't know how long the wafer would last; the look on Jenice's face showed she was thinking about that too.

'Come on. We may as well keep walking. Something about these walls might look familiar.' But at the end of the next passage there were three passageways leading away from them. Aidan groaned.

'Let's go this way,' Jenice said and she pointed to the left one. Aidan agreed for no other reason than that they were at least trying something. They had nothing with them, no compass, no string to unwind behind them to check if they were turning back on themselves. No food either, Aidan suddenly thought, as he glimpsed a shadow. He decided not to mention the shadow yet. It might have been his imagination. The knocking was still going on, a metallic sound like a small pick hitting against rock. But at the end of the passageway he saw it again: something that was there on his right side, and then when he looked properly, it wasn't. He must have made a sound for Jenice asked, 'What's wrong?'

'I think I saw something.'

Jenice looked behind her, then gave a little gasp. 'Aidan, I see them too.' She stood motionless beside him as if she'd seen a tiger snake, and Aidan turned. Just a few metres away from them were two knockers. They weren't much taller than the Lady and just as Aidan had thought before, they looked a lot like garden gnomes, except their eyes were big and bleary like the whites of eggs.

'Walk backwards,' Aidan whispered, but Jenice said, 'there are some behind us too. Lots of them.'

Aidan checked. Jenice was right — the knockers had hemmed them in.

# Twenty

'I don't think they'll hurt us.' But even as Aidan said this he wasn't sure. He just knew he couldn't run away; he had to face them. There was nowhere to run anyway. Would the knockers remember the muesli bar and let them pass? Raff had said they would.

'Keep walking, slowly.' Aidan kept his voice low. As they reached the two knockers, Jenice closed her eyes but Aidan saw them step aside to let them pass. 'They've let us through,' he whispered. 'Maybe they just wanted to look at us.'

It was an effort to stay calm, but they held hands and gently walked down the passageway to the end. Aidan looked back and he was sure he saw one of the knockers point to the left. At the end of the passageway were two more tunnels. 'Let's take the left one.'

And it was then they heard the music. It seemed like the Lady's whistle, yet it sounded so mournful, as if a violin was playing a sad, slow song. It rose all around them and when they came to the next passageway, they turned to go left again but the music blocked the way. It was as if a glass screen was there, and they couldn't pass through.

'The music is guiding us,' Jenice cried. 'Raff would say we'll be right as ninepence now.'

Aidan didn't answer. What if the music took them back to the Lady? But there was nothing he could do — the music showed the way. They emerged into a bigger passage and suddenly Aidan heard the whirring of wings — happy, excited wings.

'Raff. It's Raff!' And behind them they saw him. He flew in and landed on the ground in front of them like a magpie, wings outstretched with his heels dug into the dirt. Then he fluttered up to Aidan's shoulder. Aidan wasn't sure how to greet him. He wanted him to come but what if the Lady had sent him?

'I've come to help. You wished for me,' Raff said, breathless. 'The Lady couldn't be refusing then. Besides, when Trebiggan did not deliver you to the Lady she thought he must have eaten you after all.'

Aidan's mouth dropped open. 'But you said he didn't do that anymore.'

Raff grinned sideways at him. 'Even a pet can be turning on you of a sudden.'

'Now you tell us.'

'What about the Lady?' Jenice asked. 'Was she angry that we left?'

Raff lost his smile. 'Sad. Sad.'

'She wants you to bring us back?' Aidan knew it.

'She never thought you'd travel so far. If the giant hadn't eaten you then there be the dragaroo, though it be so brainless it doesn't know an 'A' from a duck's track. But for sure you'd get lost in the knockers' tunnels. There must be thousands of them. You could be walking forever in here.' Raff looked up at the roof of the one they were in.

'The Lady,' Aidan prompted.

'She said I could be coming to help. She sent the music so I could be finding you. She wants you to be safe, 'tis all.'

'So we can still leave Trevalia?' Aidan wanted to be sure.

'Iss, and I think we should be going, boy, before that remedy be wearing off.'

Aidan was thinking the same thing and they set off down the passageway with the music hovering like a live thing above and around them. It didn't seem so long before they reached the shaft Aidan had first come down. When they climbed out they were in the grass not far from the creek.

They decided to rest a moment but all of a sudden Raff started to flap his wings. 'Stop. Everyone back into the shaft. Oh, it has seen us, 'tis too late. Too late.'

Through his sneakers Aidan felt the ground shudder.

'What's *that*?' Jenice was holding her mouth

shut with her hands. To stop from screaming?

''Tis the dragaroo! The spriggans be leaving it here to guard their stretch of land north of the creek.'

Advancing on them was the same monster that attacked Aidan the first time he came. He'd thought about this moment a lot. As it slowly waddled towards them, the dragaroo seemed to watch Aidan, keeping its head to the side. It looked wary. Maybe its eyes were still sore from the dust he threw at it that other time.

'Do something, Raff,' Jenice shouted.

'Nothing will work. Come back now. The Lady will forgive you for leaving. Stay with us.'

Aidan frowned. 'So the Lady did tell you to try and bring us back?'

'Iss, she will welcome you back, but if you are determined to go I am still helping you.'

'Why?' Aidan looked at him sharply.

'I've grown fond, 'tis all. Come back to Trevalia. Look, the beast might be as clumsy as a cow with a musket, but 'tis dangerous. Too strong. Terrible strong.' Raff held his cap on his head with both hands and moaned.

'I'm not so sure about that.' Aidan was looking at the eucalyptus bushes behind them. What could he use? 'Dad says everything has a weak spot.'

Just then the dragaroo backed up and snorted, treading on its tail that had curled between its feet.

'Oh, spriggan spit!' Raff wailed. 'It's going to breathe fire. Run!' And he flew up ready to flee. But Aidan didn't run. Weren't eucalyptus leaves full of oil?

'Jenice, help me', he urged, and he began to pull a branch off the bush behind him. 'Quick, before that stupid thing gets its tail untangled.'

'These aren't strong enough to protect us.' Jenice pulled on one too. 'They're young and green.'

'It'll work, I hope. Just drop it when I shout. And dive when the dragaroo blows fire, okay?' Jenice grinned, suddenly catching on.

Aidan and Jenice held the branches out in front of them and crept towards the teetering dragaroo. They looked like a bush crawling along.

'Stupid, you be, boy?' Raff was suspended above them; he sounded like a little bomber, his engines revving up but going nowhere. 'How can I be keeping you safe like this?'

'It's between us and the creek,' Aidan said. 'This is all I can think of to do.'

'You can come back. Come back. That be what you can be doing.'

The dragaroo fumbled a step towards them again, managing to step over its tail this time. Warily, it stopped still and snorted some more as they came closer. So close now they could see the steam coming off the red goo dripping out of its nostrils.

Aidan could hear Raff screaming. 'You be too close! 'Tis not a game. Not a game.' Aidan kept creeping towards the dragaroo, Jenice right behind him. They were close to the dragaroo's feet. Aidan could see its scaly skin with red hairs, and its claws sticking out. He ignored Raff and kept looking up at the dragaroo's head — that way he'd be ready when it began to breathe out the fire.

But he was wrong; it was a mistake only to watch the mother. Suddenly a gaping mouth full of teeth loomed out of its pouch and a pair of claws grabbed the collar of Aidan's coat. 'Hey!' Aidan tried to push them off but they were fastened tight. He felt himself slithering up closer to the baby dragaroo.

'Aidan! Aidan. Pull your coat off!' Jenice was shouting too now.

The mother dragaroo reared backwards as the baby clung onto Aidan. 'Owww!' The claws were digging into his back right through his coat. The weight of him almost pulled the baby out of its pouch, but it wasn't letting go. All Aidan's squirming didn't get his coat off nor did it get him out of the baby dragaroo's grasp. He was slowly being dragged up towards the pouch; if they didn't do something, he'd be eaten for dinner, he knew it. And toasted first.

Why couldn't Raff do something? 'Jenice ...' Aidan tried to twist to see what she was doing. She wasn't hiding behind the bushes anymore. The branches were still in her hands and she was shoving them at the baby dragaroo.

'Let him go, you ugly monster!'

Raff dropped out of the sky like a jet bomber in a loop and brushed her head. 'Come back,

Jenice. The mother be angry. You'll be terrible burnt, all burnt to a crisp.'

But Jenice didn't stop. 'Let him go!' And she waved the branches around, just missing Aidan's head.

'It won't do any good; the dragaroo is too high.' Aidan could feel the heat on his head from the baby's jaw. Surely it didn't breathe fire too? That was when Aidan felt himself being pulled harder. His feet lifted off the ground. 'It's dragging me in!'

Jenice started jumping. One of the branches hit the baby dragaroo. It howled but continued to drag Aidan upwards. His jeans were catching on the dragaroo's scaly legs as he twisted from side to side to free himself.

Raff hovered for an instant, watching, then suddenly he pulled his cap down as far as it would go. 'Spriggan spit!' he shouted, and he dive-bombed the baby dragaroo. He poked the baby's eyes with his wings before he zoomed up again out of harm's way.

'Way to go!' shouted Jenice and Raff dived again. The baby screeched and suddenly the mother dragaroo had had enough of Raff and Jenice — it stepped back and roared.

Aidan bumped against the pouch and everyone shouted at once.

'It's going to blow,' Raff screamed.

'Drop the branches!' Aidan shouted; he squeezed his eyes shut.

Jenice squealed as she let the branches go and dived out of the way. The fire hit the ground where she'd been standing just a second before. The branches caught alight with a whoosh and Aidan felt as though he was about to fall into a bonfire. What if the baby let him go right now, onto the fire? He hung onto the rim of the pouch just in case. But the leaves were so green they didn't burn for long and soon a cloud of stinging smoke rose up and smothered both the dragaroos' noses and faces. They screeched and roared; the mother clawed at its eyes just as it had with the dust. The baby retracted its claws from Aidan's coat and disappeared into its pouch as the mother backed off, howling, into the scrub.

Aidan fell to the ground. 'Oooph.'

'Are you okay?' Jenice helped him to sit up.

'Good thinking, girl.' Raff flew onto Aidan's shoulder as the boy stood up, rubbing his eyes. The back of his neck was bleeding but otherwise he felt okay.

Jenice smiled at Raff. 'You were so brave.'

Raff hung his head. 'Not brave,' he muttered. 'Had to do something.'

Aidan grinned at Jenice and tried to joke like Raff usually did. 'Not that we would have burned too well, with our wet clothes.'

But Raff didn't laugh, just made a noise with his tongue. ''Twas too close. Terrible close, and smoke won't be keeping them away for long.'

That decided Jenice. 'Perhaps we should be going now.' She kissed Raff's cheek. That made him chuckle, but his face went as red as the draga-roo's fire.

'Please come back and visit,' he said, laughing again and flying in the air beside them as they jogged towards the creek. 'We'd all be happy as ducks if you did. We may be needing more of your help one day.'

Aidan stopped running. 'I don't think I'll be coming back,' he said carefully. He looked up and saw the creek close by. The old rusted 'danger' sign was skew-whiff on its post. That sign was true at least — it was definitely dangerous to cross the creek.

Raff looked almost sly. 'One never knows what be around the corner. I could be coming with you.'

Jenice quickly glanced at Aidan, a frown in place. 'I don't think so,' Aidan said firmly. 'My friends wouldn't understand.'

'They wouldn't see me unless they had magic ointment in their eyes.'

'He'd be too much trouble,' Jenice whispered.

Aidan agreed but he knew he'd never forget Raff all the same. 'Thank you for all your help,' he said, and Raff flew to his shoulder one more time and hugged him around the neck. Then he hovered in the air and watched, as Aidan took Jenice's hand.

''Bye,' Raff called. From a distance, his voice sounded like water splashing into a fountain. ''Bye, 'bye, 'bye.'

Aidan and Jenice waved, then they turned to face the creek. Aidan placed his foot firmly on the first stone. 'You ready?' he asked. For a moment he felt the cold quiver in his stomach again. It was weird — when the baby dragaroo was dragging him into its pouch he didn't have time to feel those shivers in his stomach. But now, with time to think, it was different — what if Josie and Raff were wrong and Jenice had been gone too long? What would happen?

Jenice smiled at Aidan's question. 'Yes,' and she put a foot on the next stone. They were stepping across the stones carefully and Aidan was starting to breathe more easily when just before they reached the other side, Jenice's foot slipped. She reeled against Aidan, making him teeter to one side. He regained his balance and, fortunately, he was still holding her hand and managed to keep her from landing in the water. Aidan didn't want to think about what might happen if Jenice fell in a second time.

'You okay?' he asked.

'I think so. I feel so weird. Everything's rushing around me, like I'm on a ride at the show that's going too fast.'

'Here, just hang on to me — there's only one stone to go.' Aidan pulled Jenice after him, and helped her scramble up the bank of the creek. She put her head on her knees and sat on the grass by the 'Keep Out' sign. Aidan sat watching her, not daring to say anything. What if the timing was wrong? What if she died?

Finally she looked up at Aidan. 'It's gone.'

'You'll be right now?' Aidan bit his lip.

Jenice grinned. 'As right as ninepence.'

Aidan put out his hand to help her up and they started up the gravel track to the town. He wondered what Mrs Trengove was going to say when he turned up at her door with Jenice. He hoped she wouldn't faint.

# Epilogue

*Light News* 23 May

## Miracle in the Mine

JENICE TRENGOVE, who disappeared last year near the mine creek and was thought to be lost down a mineshaft or drowned, arrived in the town yesterday with Aidan Curnow who has been missing for three weeks. Both children were wet through as though they had been swimming. Police suspected that Aidan had been kidnapped, and Mr Curnow had made an appearance on national TV appealing to the kidnappers to reveal the whereabouts of his son. Mr Curnow claimed that Aidan would not have drowned in the creek as he was a strong swimmer for his age and a member of the rowing club before the creek was closed to the public last year.

Apparently the children have been asleep since their return but are currently undergoing tests and counselling regarding their ordeal. When asked about Jenice's return, Mrs Trengove was overcome with emotion. She is a widow and Jenice is her only child. 'It's like having your child brought back to life. It's a miracle,' was her only comment. Mr and Mrs Curnow were both emotional when questioned about the disappearance of their son. Mr Curnow made no comment about the children's whereabouts, even though it appears they had been in the mine for a year and three weeks respectively. Doctor Bernard Quinn told reporters today that Jenice had probably suffered heatstroke, which can cause delusions and she had forgotten how to go home. No one seems to have the answers to the many questions that arise from this theory. How did the children stay alive?

ROBERT GEORGE

*Light News* 30 May

# Writing Changed on Fountain

AT AN assembly at the primary school yesterday, the mayor unveiled a new plaque on the fountain. The fountain was erected six months after the disappearance of Jenice Trengove, bearing the inscription: *In memory of Jenice Trengove, who was lost in the bush but never lost to us.* Today these words were added: *And in tribute to Aidan Curnow who found her alive and well.* The principal presented Aidan and Jenice with medals for bravery. Although the details of their disappearance remain obscure, it is obvious that they must both have endured great hardship, especially Aidan who has scars from gashes on his upper back and neck.

Afterwards at morning tea, reporter Anna Calley offered Aidan Curnow a plate of fairy bread. He looked at the triangles of buttered bread with hundreds and thousands and said, 'That isn't true fairy bread.'

'It should be made with fruit,' added Jenice Trengove who was sitting next to him.

Mrs Trengove overheard and commented that the children had always liked fairy bread, after which, both the children took some, but their smiles seemed to conceal some shared secret.

In Celtic literature true fairy bread is made of fruit, but how did the children know this? Will we ever discover what happened to these children who were lost in the mine across the creek?

ANNA-MAY CALLEY

# A Note from the Author

A **piskey** is a Cornish fairy. They can be very mischievous, luring people into difficult situations, and playing tricks. They also laugh a lot. The Cornish had a great belief in piskeys. If travellers lost their way they were said to be 'piskey-led'; people thought piskeys led folks astray with lights that looked like lanterns. It was believed some went 'beyond the seas' and I built this story upon that idea. What if they had come with the Cornish people who came to South Australia in the 1840s to work in the mines at Kapunda and Burra, then later at Moonta?

Then I read about the Lost Child of St Allen. This is a Cornish story of a boy who was lost. When he was found he told everyone how he was lured by music into a dark grove and found himself at the edge of a lake. A beautiful lady led him to an underground cavern that was built of crystal and supported by glass pillars. I thought maybe this was what happened to Jenice Trengove.

The **small people** were said to be spirits of an ancient Cornish race. They help people they like, enjoy dancing and wear colourful clothes, the men usually wearing green, with a blue jacket and a three-cornered cap, sometimes with a feather in it. A **browney** was a kind and good household fairy who helped the family with whom it lived.

**Spriggans** were a race of warrior fairies, grotesquely ugly, who could alter their size at will. They were guardians of buried treasure and also lured children away. I decided to make them the ones in this story to lure people away with lights like lanterns, hence the jack-o'-lanterns — one name for the marsh lights caused by the burning of natural gases.

The **knockers** were the little people who lived underground in the mines. And, yes, there was a Cornish **giant** called **Trebiggan**. He had long arms that could pluck men from passing ships, and it was said he dined on young humans fried on a large flat rock near his cave.

The Aboriginal spirits in the story were the ones that the Ngadjuri people believed in.

Did you guess I made up the dragaroo? I combined an Australian animal with one from folklore.

# Sources

In writing *Across the Creek* I found the following works helpful:

Bettelheim, B., *The Uses of Enchantment*. London: Thames and Hudson, 1975

Briggs, K., *The Fairies in Tradition and Literature*. London: Routledge & Kegan Paul, 1967

Deane, T. & Shaw T., *The Folklore of Cornwall*. London: BT Batsford, 1975

Hawke, K., *Cornish Sayings, Superstitions and Remedies*. St Austell, Cornwall: K. Hawke, 1973

Hunt, R., *The Drolls, Traditions and Superstitions of Old Cornwall* (1881). Felinfach: Llanerch Publishers, 1993

Knight, F., Anderson, S. & Pring, A., *The Ngadjuri People of the Mid North of South Australia: walpa juri*, in press.